31
MILES

Vinita Bakshi is an award winning sociologist and social entrepreneur. She is an alumnus of prestigious Delhi School of Economics.

She has founded a nonprofit organization- AAMBRA Foundation, with a vision towards women empowerment and skill development. She is the chief architect and brain behind, She Speaks, a seminar series dealing with the issues faced by the contemporary South Asian women. She is also the Founder of AAMBROTSAVE, an annual cultural festival which brings to the fore not only Literature but also the visual and performing arts, crafts, cuisines, weaves and many waning traditions of India. She is currently serving as Director of National Institute of Jewellery (NIJ), Delhi.

Vinita has a passion for literature and writes fiction and non-fiction, bilingually in English and Hindi. She has also published papers on gender and feminism.

31 MILES

CAN WE EVER WIN
AGAINST OURSELVES?

VINITA BAKSHI

RUPA

Published by
Rupa Publications India Pvt. Ltd 2016
7/16, Ansari Road, Daryaganj
New Delhi 110002

Sales centres:
Allahabad Bengaluru Chennai
Hyderabad Jaipur Kathmandu
Kolkata Mumbai

ISBN: 978-81-291-4229-0

First impression 2016

10 9 8 7 6 5 4 3 2 1

Contents

Part II

Foreword

To the reader of this book,

I'm asked to write a lot of foreword of books. I mostly refuse. Not because the author is not known to me, or that the work is terrible. I refuse because I don't see anything different or unique in that work. I am a sceptic by nature and usually seek something out of the ordinary in a fairly mediocre and conventional world. Thus when I was asked to write the foreword of this book, the same lack of conviction and search for something unique was first on my mind. The fact that I've written the foreword is proof enough that I found it.

That's my part of why I wrote this opening. Now comes your part, the reader who is right now on this foreword. Let me try and guess what you're thinking right now. Why would a TV show host and a Technology Journalist write a foreword to a book like this. Well, the answer lies in the question. It's because 'it's a book like this'. I've always been fascinated by good stories, tales that transform you to lands unknown and make you meet people you've never met before. To lose yourself in their lives, their universe, their events and happenings - is magical. That's the magic I felt as I started on my journey of *31 Miles*. It's the magic you are about to feel.

31 Miles is a rare gem; a layered journey of a middle-aged, traditionalist called Mansa, written by debutant author, sociologist, and activist Vinita Bakshi. In our popular imagination, the word magic is usually associated with the lives of younger urban women, in particular millennials, who by virtue of living in a globalized and relatively more liberal South Asia, can afford to enjoy higher levels of freedom, and bend if not break convention.

Mansa's story is one of self-discovery, of the intellectual, physical and metaphysical spheres, and how their cross-section changes the life of the protagonist forever.

That being said, *31 Miles* provides a riveting and candid commentary on the dynamics of a rapidly modernizing urban Indian society and the aspirations of its members—women, men, the young and the old. As you join Mansa, I invite you the audience, to read between the lines, to discover a world steeped in tradition, mysticism and ritual which blends, albeit not always seamlessly, with rationality and westernization.

The themes in this book are omnipresent in the lives of modern Indians; the reader will quite often find a reflection of themselves or that of a loved one, or acquaintances in the pages of this narrative.

Yet, the concept of the everyday hero who exists in the ethos of the midlife, bourgeois woman has not been dealt with the right sensitivity in India's popular media, art or literature.

The author has vast experience working for women's rights

and empowerment, which has brought her in contact with hundreds of individuals who aspire to emancipate themselves economically and socially using channels of education, awareness and work ethic. I can infer from my discourses with Vinita, that the protagonist of *31 Miles*—Mansa has been conceived as a unification of these experiences.

I commend Vinita for the uniqueness of this book's theme and highly recommend *31 Miles* for its fascinating narrative, valiant characters and most importantly the call for self-discovery.

It's time for you to start your journey of *31 Miles*. I promise you an amazing adventure of the mind and heart.

Rajiv Makhni
Thursday, 5 February 2015

Prologue
Here Begins the Story

THE BRIGHT SUN overhead, despite the canopy on the boat, made the pain sharper and caused Mansa to feel dizzier. Mansa had insisted to take the centuries-old traditional boat instead of a motorboat, leaving Abhijit with little choice in the matter.

It took them over an hour of rowing to reach the confluence of the River Ganga, River Yamuna and the mythical River Saraswati. Despite her pain, Mansa appeared brighter and radiated a sense of happiness, which Abhijit had not seen in ages. He extended his hand to help her stand.

Mansa wanted Abhijit to go into the water first, and so he jumped into the river. Finally, holding on to the boatman with one hand and gripping Abhijit tightly with the other, she alighted from the boat. Abhijit held her hands, and chanting shlokas and mantras, they took several dips together.

Mansa appeared exhausted after the dips. Holding her firmly and looking skyward, Abhijit prayed, 'Oh God, let Mansa be my wife for all my lives.'

Mansa looked at him in disbelief. A man who could never even bring himself to say 'I love you' earlier, had said it all today. A pall of guilt enveloped her. Mansa felt scared and nervous, as she secretly wanted to pray for Rajan's prosperity and happiness, as she still thought of him as her true love. Whatever his intentions or feelings had been, the fact was that she had loved him passionately and truthfully.

She was seeing the same emotions mirrored in Abhijit's eyes for her. Suddenly, she felt giddy and her grip on Abhijit's hand loosened. The boat by now had drifted a little further away. Holding her tight, Abhijit tried wading towards the boat. The level of the water started rising too. As Abhijit reached the boat, the boatman tried to balance and straighten the boat. Abhijit had no choice but to get in first, so he could help Mansa into the boat. Firmly holding the edges, he hoisted himself into it. He reached out and took Mansa's hand. Suddenly, another boat collided with theirs, shaking their boat violently. Abhijit's grip on Mansa's hand loosened.

Mansa fell into the water. As she fell, Guru Ma's words echoed in her ears: 'For the Kaal Chakra to be broken, you will have to be saved by one of the two men from your previous life and you will have to die a natural death.'

Part I

1

Rainbow Days

'Out beyond ideas of wrongdoing and right doing, there is a field. I'll meet you there.'

—Rumi

IT WAS A bright May morning. Abhijit woke up—again—with unpleasant memories of his nightmare. His shirt was damp, even though the room was as cold as a winter's night with only the air conditioner's dull hum breaking the absolute stillness of the room. The childhood nightmare had taken deep root, spreading itself steadily and firmly into his subconscious:

It is twilight. He stands anxiously awaiting his bus amidst the ocean of people. A dilapidated bus approaches the bus stop, causing the usual mayhem. Abhijit is preparing to board. The bus halts and a few people get in but as soon as he tries boarding the bus, there is a vicious push from inside and he is thrown out. He quickly recovers from the shock, and desperately runs after the bus. While chasing it, he notices an old man sitting in the last seat. The man suddenly turns his head, laughing jubilantly and mockingly at Abhijit.

Abhijit woke up screaming only to find solace in Mansa's arms, with his head resting on her bosom. Abhijit and Mansa, both troubled souls, one suffering from nightmares and the other often struck by crippling headaches, were brought together by their families and declared as two people best suited for each other. Years had passed, life was wonderful, but their troubles continued to haunt them.

Abhijit was dusky, with sharp aristocratic features, and was taller than Mansa. He was considered to be very handsome by his family and circle of friends. He had solid academic credentials, with an impeccable reputation as a scientist par excellence, heading many key international projects while working for various multinational corporations. He had a presence, which was inspiring rather than intimidating. But for his wife, Mansa, he was even more valuable than that.

Abhijit had grown up in a small town. However, his progressive thinking and respect for women, coupled with unmatched intelligence, had made him the epitome of perfection in Mansa's eyes. Mansa had spent her entire 20s and 30s admiring and idolizing him. She took pride in herself for having the best husband.

They had been living in Mumbai when Mansa had been pregnant with Shonali. The mornings would be noisy, with the bustle of vehicles, cars honking in their residential complex, the continuous sound of the old OTIS lifts stopping on their floor, and the maid ranting about having to wash too many breakfast utensils. On one such morning, as Abhijit was about to leave for office and Mansa was seeing him off at the door, she suddenly dropped the car keys on the floor. As she was about to bend to pick up the keys, Abhijit shouted, startling everyone around, 'Why are you bending? Don't you know that in your state it's not right to bend? It could harm you or even the baby!'

Mansa, grinning, replied, 'Don't you know you should not scream around a pregnant woman? You could have frightened the baby too.'

The maid also came running from the kitchen, but Abhijit had quickly bent down to retrieve the keys before Mansa could. Their daughter Malvika had keenly observed this; and her innocent mind thought that Mom was probably not supposed to bend, so Malvika would imitate her father. She could not comprehend that after Shonali was born, Mansa did not need to exercise such extreme caution. Shonali also grew up observing what happened when Mom tried to reach out for something. She also instinctively developed the habit of reaching out and bending before Mansa could. Thus, she had people trying to outdo her from three directions. She always smiled to see such lavish concern. It was because Abhijit practiced what he preached that both her girls also doted on her so much.

Ever since she could recollect, life had been kind to her. The youngest of three sisters, she had been her father's princess and had always effortlessly got whatever she desired. If ever her father refused her anything, then there was her Dadi, her doting paternal grandmother and closest ally, who would do anything for the three sisters, and especially for her.

In her parent's home, she had been indulged, given all the comforts of life. Yet the sisters were far from being spoilt. Her ever-obliging parents and Dadi not only provided them with the best of everything in material terms but also created a balance with a very strong set of values so as to lay a foundation for the sisters to be sensible, responsible, and caring. All three sisters were brought up on the teachings of the Bhagavad Gita, Puranas, Ramayana and Mahabharata. Truth, morality, and an emphasis on good character were the values expected to be followed by most upper middle class households of that time without sermonizing.

During her youth and even after her marriage, Mansa's main entertainment was being glued to the television when epic series like *The Ramayana* and the *Mahabharata* were aired. Mansa's choices were formed and influenced by the family culture of migrant Punjabi Hindus, who had made Delhi their permanent home since the partition of India in 1947. Movies had also interested her a great deal, besides the usual dose of soppy Mills & Boons.

Every Monday and Tuesday, she would visit a nearby temple with her group of friends. On their way, they would discuss newly released movies, their favourite serials and recently read books. The daily soap culture was still relatively new to India then so the latest Mills & Boon was the point of discussion, especially the hero who would invariably be tall, dark and handsome.

Mansa was still pursuing her Master's degree, when her parents had decided that it was time for her to get married. Since she had never dated, her answer had been a meek, shy smile. A brief customary meeting with Abhijit had been set up at their home; although, unknown to them, the family elders had already fixed their marriage and sealed their fates.

That had been a significant day in the life of the Jaitly family, when Abhijit was visiting them for the first time. Mansa's mother had asked her to wear her prettiest orange and green churidar-kurta for the special occasion. Mansa had felt a little intimidated and excited at the same time. Her mother had given Mansa her very own big, intricate filigree gold jhumkis, which she had always thought would look most engaging on her youngest daughter. Mansa was slimmer than her sisters and looked barely sixteen so her mother thought the earrings would serve the twin purpose of making her daughter look prettier and mature.

Mansa had stood before a mirror staring spellbound at herself. She had barely any opportunity to wear such stuff before. Although, when her parents were not around Mansa had seen her sisters indulge in a fashion parade with their mother's jewellery, saris and scarlet lipstick, but she had never participated in these escapades. Firstly, being the youngest she was hardly left alone at home and secondly, her father and Dadi strongly resented her trying any Indian outfits in the belief that if she was kept away from those, she would remain a child. Even when Mansa had grown out of her skirts and frocks, they were not ready to accept the fact that she was growing up. Once when Mansa had passed out of her senior secondary school, she recalled how her mother had very lovingly stitched a salwar-kurta for her, but her father and Dadi firmly insisted that Mansa was too young for such outfits and saris yet.

As these incidents played on her mind, Mansa proudly admired her new look and shook her head from side to side to see how the jhumkis glittered and complemented her perfect oval face.

When she met Abhijit, the only question Abhijit had asked her was, 'Mansa, what was your senior secondary percentage?'

'Sixty-five per cent,' Mansa had replied shyly.

'I scored much higher marks!' Abhijit had exclaimed.

Mansa had lowered her head and felt terrified, lest he asked her what her graduation percentage was. She had tried to collect her thoughts, but blurted out, 'Yes, because science is more scoring.'

Abhijit had ignored her response, and then jumped to enquire about her graduation score.

Mansa, nervously gathering her hair on one side, had replied, 'Almost 60 per cent. I missed 60 by only two marks.' She felt the same heartache regarding the devastating tragedy of her marks not reaching the standard benchmark of 60 per cent—as she always did.

To her pleasant surprise, no more questions were asked, although the family elders had warned that Abhijit may ask about her cooking and housekeeping skills. Mansa's mother had constantly coached her, 'Don't feel shaky and face him confidently.' Thus, she had been prepared to face Abhijit as an apprentice is trained to go through an interview, but was relieved she had not been asked about domestic chores.

After Abhijit left, her mother had immediately exclaimed, 'What a noble family—how fortunate Mansa is!'

As it was summer time and her exams were going on,

it was decided by both families that they would be formally engaged first and then fix the wedding on the earliest astrologically suitable date—which turned out to be a few months later.

Mansa and Abhijit never took advantage of the intermittent time to meet or to understand each other. They were never left alone to strike up a conversation. Her elder sister, Mala, who was a rebel and had a love marriage with a boy from the neighbourhood, much against her parents' wishes, had found Abhijit's lack of interest in Mansa quite queer. She did not understand why Abhijit had not once tried meeting Mansa alone or why he had not taken his fiancée out on a date.

Mala, a champion in her own right, telephoned Abhijit and told him, 'You must treat all three of us to a dinner; you are getting married to the prettiest of us all.' Her girlie giggles on the phone were so mischievous that Abhijit had been shaken out of his mould. He instantly replied, 'Why not? Whenever you say, Mala!'

Mala was triumphant. 'Tomorrow night,' she had declared.

Abhijit had agreed with a meek reply, 'Yes sure, tomorrow night.'

Rolling with laughter and like a true victor, she had then announced to Meera and Mansa, 'Guess what? Abhijit is taking us all for dinner tomorrow.'

Mansa had been shocked. 'Did he call you?'

'No! I called him. So what? What difference does it make?'

Mansa couldn't help feeling embarrassed and angry, as she had thought that it was up to Abhijit to have thought of taking her out for dinner.

'Oh Maladi, you will never change!' she had wailed in irritation.

'Why should I change?' Mala had asked, 'You're such a Papa's pet. It's you who needs to change. Stop hiding at home. Go out and see how much the world has changed. You were always the Dadi "chipkoo". You should thank me. I made the effort, thinking Abhijit would open up, and both of you would get to know each other before your marriage. Someone needed to push him on the right track. I couldn't control my laughter when he asked about your marks, instead of your interests and trying to get to know you. Instead of thanking me, you are giving me gyaan!'

Her plan had worked, and Abhijit had taken them out for dinner. But even after that, he had not made any effort to reach out to Mansa even with a phone call.

Mala wondered out loud, 'Does he have another love interest and is being forced to marry or is he generally so unsociable? Looks like that he is more of a tubelight than you are!'

Mansa's belief that her parents always did and would do the best for her, along with the excitement of creating a wedding trousseau, happily egged her on into matrimony. She never gave a thought about the responsibilities a marriage entails. As the final college semester rolled in, a vague desire to appear for the Indian Civil Services exam surfaced, since most of her classmates were preparing for the prestigious entrance exams. However, that desire ebbed rather easily by the flow of ritual shopping, and the other excitements that come with the grandiose north Indian wedding.

Before the wedding and during the wedding rituals, Mansa was very anxious about being alone with Abhijit; after all, she barely knew him. And then on the wedding night, nervous and decked up in her bridal finery, she had been left to wait for him in a room adorned with mogra flowers, reminding her of the Bollywood suhag raat scenes.

Numb and fearful, she had sat like an inert bundle recalling tips and advice about how to deal with the awkward moments of spending the first night of marriage with a complete stranger. Fear had made her forget all her cues but luckily Abhijit had turned out to be rather gentle; and she discovered that even though they were strangers, they had a lot to talk about. He had spent the first few nights just holding and caressing her while they shared stories of their childhood and youth. There had been incessant laughter as they recalled the silly childhood memories. In these moments, Mansa found she could trust him. She had even told him about the deadly morning when she had experienced a head-shattering migraine for the first time as a child. However, she couldn't share her painful experience when her schoolmates bullied her, calling her a dumbo.

Abhijit, too, told her about his recurrent nightmares, saying that perhaps they would disappear since he had found his soulmate in her, and felt lucky to be married to someone so pretty. Abhijit also had great stories to share of his academic credentials and heroic sporting feats. Mansa, already in awe of him, had listened intently as he spoke of his achievements. Together, they enjoyed making fun of Bollywood's over-emotive and dramatic love scenes, especially the suhag raat scenes. Mansa blindly trusted that he had as clean a past as she did. It was only after a fortnight that they consummated their relationship. They had felt extremely fortunate to have each other and were thankful to their parents for having found such likeminded and compatible partners for them.

Mansa's pampering continued as Abhijit always made sure that all her needs and comforts were taken care of. Mansa appreciated his attentiveness, but sometimes felt that mostly his actions stemmed from a sense of duty and less out of love. Still, sinking into the comforts of domestic lethargy with a caring husband, supportive in-laws, loving parents and doting sisters was easy.

2

New Delhi Times

> 'A life without love is of no account. Don't ask yourself what kind of love you should seek, spiritual or material, divine or mundane, Eastern or Western. Love has no labels, no definitions. Love is the water of life. And a lover is a soul of fire! The universe turns differently when fire loves water.'
>
> —Elif Shafak

SEASONS AND CALENDARS had changed and almost two decades had passed by peacefully, but once the children grew up and needed her less, Mansa began losing interest in everything. She could not understand why she developed misgivings about her current state of affairs after all these years. Boredom had caused many visible changes in her. She repeatedly asked herself why her life had become so predictably mundane. Abhijit and Shonali complained that she had started talking to herself and nagging them constantly.

One morning, as Abhijit was about to leave for office, Mansa was in one of her usual grumpy moods, 'It's getting so boring being at home day after day. I don't know what to do!'

'Mrs Pathak is in town,' Abhijit informed her, 'Go visit her. Join her kitty group or go see an exhibition or a play. If you want, I will get movie tickets in the evening. I am getting late now. Let me know over the phone which movie you want to see.'

Seeing Mansa sulk despite all his offers, Abhijit added, 'We can even go shopping in the evening if you like.' Bidding her a hurried goodbye, he left the house. Mansa had not even budged from the dining chair, leave alone opening her mouth for a decent farewell.

An empty house stared back at her. No Abhijit and no Shonali. Malvika was away pursuing higher studies abroad. She cast a glance full of loathing in the direction of the television, newspapers and magazines, and then crashed headlong on the bed, sinking her face into the mattress, her tears rolling down.

Mansa did not understand why she was not interested in hanging out with her kitty friends any more or even catching up with the latest movies. Abhijit's overtly attentive nature now seemed to smother her. She had herself happily chosen to be a homemaker, while the man of the house took care of the rest. Abhijit had pretty much done that—he had steadily risen and served in the National Nuclear Research Institute (NNRI), Surat, in a very senior capacity. Only a couple of months back, Abhijit had joined as the Chief Operations Officer of a Gurgaon-based MNC, which had earlier been NNRI's knowledge partner. His pay packet was a considerable amount. Despite the comfort he had given her, Mansa felt disoriented and was consumed with boredom.

For two decades, Mansa had prided herself on being the best cook, a caring wife, a loving mother, a good hostess and a daughter-in-law par excellence. She had thoroughly enjoyed and done complete justice to these roles, duties and responsibilities. She wondered, what was different now?

She had succeeded in keeping the mid-thirties' blues and bulges away and had been extremely popular in her limited kitty circle. *Then suddenly, why is this emptiness growing in me? Why this pain after so many years? Why am I not able to accept myself as I am*, she thought. Perhaps the calamity lay in the fact that she did not know who she was any more. All her roles seemed to have reached their destined points.

She thought of her married life, how her role as a wife still continued. Mansa and Abhijit had always agreed that love was an imaginary emotion in prose and poetry, and was best suited to the celluloid world. To the best of Mansa's knowledge, she was the first woman in Abhijit's life, and Abhijit was definitely the first man in hers. They had happily chosen the arranged marriage route.

As she lay crying into her pillow, some bitter memories from school resurfaced. She must have been in class eleven. She had entered the classroom enthusiastically, but could sense there was a spicy gossip session going on. As soon as her classmates saw her, the energy of the classroom changed from fun and laughter to an uncomfortable silence and a boy stood up and announced, 'Hey, Ms Dumbo is here.' A girl quipped, 'Oh no, not again, please…call her Ms Bore please…suits her better!' And most of the girls of her class, even her so-called close friends, burst into wicked laughter. Not knowing why she was the subject of this ridicule, she had run out of the class in tears. At such times, she could only confide in God. She felt lucky that at least one of her friends, Madhulika, never slighted her. In college too, her friends often called her primitive, Stone Aged and judgmental snob, as she had a strong, conventional moral code. However, she always prided herself on the fact that she was a one-man woman, who had never dated anyone before or after marriage and there was nothing in the world that could ever change that. She couldn't figure out why such an old memory was affecting her so.

At times she had felt bad that she might have missed out in life due to her over-protective parents and husband, who kept her bubble-wrapped against the harsh realities of the world.

She pushed herself off the bed and wandered to the veranda. The vast expanse of the greenery around did not soothe her mind. She did not know what she was looking for. She rested her hands on the railing, lamenting that if she did not do something soon the boredom would kill her completely. Time was slipping through her fingers. Malvika had left to pursue dentistry in London, Shonali was busy with her curriculum and coaching for the ninth class, while Abhijit spent long, tiring days at work. She had spent her life educating her young children, looking after her and Abhijit's old parents, but it was Abhijit who bought their house and saved his hard-earned money for their old age. Maybe she could help do something now for herself and contribute to the old-age plans.

Incidentally, Mansa's arrival in Gurgaon after Abhijit joined the new company had led to her chance meetings and interactions with people around her own age group. They more or less had the same academic background as Mansa, but were now CEOs, civil servants, writers, or other professionals established in their own right, which filled her with regret. The only things she achieved were an experience-bank of drivers, maids, gardeners, and at best, kitty party women friends. She felt embarrassed and left out when she interacted with them.

Once settled in Gurgaon, she joined a gym in the vicinity of her new home. On her first morning, as she was exploring the new space and admiring the state-of-the-art equipment, she was pleasantly surprised to hear her name called out.

'Hey Mansa… is it really you?'

Mansa turned around and exclaimed, 'It's you, Chhaya! I don't believe this. Oh my God!'

And they both stared incredulously at each other. Chhaya had been in her class in college, although they had never been thick friends. But meeting an old college classmate had filled them both with warmth.

'My, you look so different,' Mansa had said.

'Look at you! No signs of change. Have you gone under the knife or something?'

Mansa had failed to grasp the implication, and had naively replied, 'No, no! I am completely healthy and very regular with my diet and exercise.'

Chhaya's eyes twinkled, 'So I see. But where had you vanished all these years? You are not even part of the college network or any group. We even tried looking for you online. Why all the secrecy, dear?'

Mansa adroitly diverted the conversation, for she had no

clue how to respond to what Chhaya was saying. Online? Well, she was not really tech-savvy. Keeping the conversation going on safer topics, she had quickly asked, 'How many children do you have?'

'Oh, I have a son. Thirteen. And you?'

'I have two lovely daughters. Fifteen and twenty-one,' a proud Mansa replied.

Chhaya was surprised, 'Gosh…now who is going to believe that you have a daughter who is twenty-one years old? Oh yes, you were almost the first one to be married in the class, while we all prepared for our civil service exams. I even remember attending your wedding—but we didn't hear from you since then.'

Mansa muttered that her family, children and the move to a new city had taken up most of her time. Chhaya thought that Mansa had a transferable job and when Mansa had corrected her, saying that it was her husband's job that took them to new places every few years, Chhaya had curiously asked what she did for a living.

Mansa felt mortified to admit she was a plain homemaker. But she laughingly said that at least she was a free bird. Chhaya, ever so tactfully said, 'Oh, hats off to you. Some people unnecessarily underestimate homemakers. It is the most difficult job in the world, I tell you. Though I couldn't stay at home and be entirely domestic, it has its own pleasures and pains. Look at us…careers and work make life so much more complicated; we had to work out a ten-year plan before we could think of having Krish.'

Mansa was not sure if Chhaya's comment was sarcastic or not. However, she smilingly asked, 'So you are a civil servant?'

'No, no! Vikram is. My current husband. But he is not Krish's father. Long story. Will tell you some other time. To answer your question, I write. I write on technology and have two books published till now.'

'Technology? Books published? Oh, that's really awesome. But you aren't an engineer?' Mansa asked.

Chhaya laughed, saying, 'Re-invent, Mansa. In with the new and out with the old!' She asked Mansa to get back in touch with their classmates, winking and telling her how all the guys still remembered her. Then she left.

After talking to Chhaya, Mansa felt as though she was some relic from the past. Although in Surat, where they had been stationed earlier, Mansa had been considered the coolest amongst her kitty friends; but in Gurgaon she felt unable to forge an identity of her own.

Looking around the gym, she spotted a vacant treadmill and began her workout, noticing that the clientele consisted of stylish, sophisticated people. At 9 a.m., many men and women who were discussing stock prices, politics or international affairs while they worked out, started heading towards the shower and change rooms. She looked at them in awe when they emerged impeccably and formally dressed, ready for office. She gawked enviously at them as the idea of heading back home only to meet Bela, her maid, and the idiot box filled her with dread.

All the people around her were career-driven intellectuals, a tribe she now desperately wanted to belong to. She wanted to begin somewhere, however small, even though age was not on her side and her qualifications were as historical as she was.

When she reached home, Abhijit had already left for office,

just as he did every day. Almost six long months had passed since they had shifted to Gurgaon from Surat. And every passing day was just getting worse, adding to her misery.

Dragging her feet glumly to the main hall, Mansa reached for the newspaper. There, splattered in huge letters in the paper, was an advertisement by a celebrity chef inviting applications for a cooking course. Though routine cooking tested her patience to the hilt now, she knew she enjoyed creating new delicacies. It sounded interesting but she abandoned the idea, thinking she could not go back to cooking again. As the day progressed, she decided to go through the advertisement again. This time it sounded promising and attractive. The only drawback was that it was expensive and she wondered if Abhijit would agree to her joining it.

Nevertheless, she decided that she would ask Abhijit and enrol for the programme. When she did, Abhijit was most encouraging. She felt happy and looked forward to joining the classes. Abhijit was just happy to see her interested in something after a very long time; he was not able to make sense of the despair she had drowned in.

3

Born Again

'Rummaging in our souls, we often dig up something that ought to have lain there unnoticed.'

—Leo Tolstoy

IT WAS MANSA'S first morning as a student at her gourmet-cooking class. She had not felt this exhilarated in years. The course was for six-week—five days a week, five hours a day. A celebrity chef from a five-star hotel was conducting the course. Mansa knew that when combined with commuting and getting ready, it would become a full-day affair.

In her excitement, Mansa had spent the previous night eagerly waiting for the morning to arrive. Abhijit had tried calming her but nothing worked. They made love, but Mansa could count the minutes till it would last. She knew exactly where Abhijit's hand would move next.

In her excitement about the upcoming class, she had fallen

asleep only at dawn. When her alarm buzzed at 6 a.m., her automatic response was to strangulate it. She covered her head with her pillow, groaning. The golden sunshine coming through her green window drapes caressed her face, waking her with a start. She realized it was 7.45 a.m., and then it hit her. The course began at 9 sharp! Quickly, she sat up in bed, and saw Abhijit leisurely reading the newspaper, his mug of black coffee in his hand. She noticed the pot of tea that the maid usually left at her bedside table at 6.15 a.m., cold as tap-water now. Mansa scuttled towards the bathroom without drinking her customary cup of tea. She went straight under the shower, not bothering with the temperature of the water. One hand was on the shower knob, while the other vigorously brushing her teeth.

She thanked her stars that she had arranged her clothes the night before. She had also washed and styled her long hair the previous day. There was a time when she took no time at all to dress, as she typically wore jeans and well-fitted tops with minimal jewellery, her make-up consisting of just kohl and peach gloss to accentuate her best features.

Over the years, she had accumulated a remarkable collection of bags, watches and shoes, which she couldn't do without. All she wanted when she travelled abroad was to gaze at Jimmy Choos and Ferragamos, lucky to have a doting husband, who would unquestioningly give her money to buy them. Today was no day to fuss over shoes and bags, she thought while fastening her watch and dabbing a bit of Magie Noire behind her ears. She was all set to leave in half an hour.

As she left her bedroom, the aroma of curry leaves in sambhar filled her nostrils. Her usual reaction would have been to ask for a bowl to taste it before it reached the dining table, but today she suppressed the urge in favour of her lip shimmer. She asked Bela for a sandwich, which she could eat in the car on her way to class, along with a travel coffee mug. She scampered to the drawing room first to check if Abhijit had everything he needed and then to Shonali, who was still in bed as the summer vacation was on.

Once out, she realized that Sanjay, her driver, hadn't come, causing her to panic again. She wondered if she should just drive herself but knew that Abhijit would not allow her to drive, and if she persisted he would waste a lot of time warning and lecturing her against the hazards of driving in the NCR. She knew he would also offer to drop her, even though it would mean that he would get late, but she didn't want to be over-dependent on him on her first day itself.

She threw caution to the wind and gestured to Bela to bring her the car keys and paced towards the road, while the other maid followed her with her laptop and snack box. She refused the snack box and grabbed the laptop. She got into the car, initially driving hesitantly, but soon she was humming Queen's 'Break Free' and felt adrenaline course through her veins.

Of course she was late, and when she reached the third floor after hastily parking her car, it was already 9.30 a.m. Striding hurriedly, she pushed the heavy metal-encrusted, squeaky wooden door to peep into the conference room, embarrassed when the lecture stopped and all heads swung in her direction.

There were about a dozen students, men and women, all stylish and rich. The lecture was being delivered by a stocky man of middling height, who looked as though he was born to only eat and drink. He was wearing an expensive watch and had a strong foreign accent. He gestured her towards an empty place with a placard that had 'Neena' written on it. She perched herself on the empty chair, feeling like she didn't belong there. The chef resumed his lecture soon after the brief interruption.

She found herself surveying the alien surroundings. She was at the far end of the room, with the door diagonally behind her. The tapestry and drapes were all black and white with a business-like elegance. Names of some exotic herbs were displayed on the white screen, so Mansa felt that she hadn't missed much, maybe just the round of introductions.

On her desk lay a black folder with a pen, pencil, eraser and study material tucked inside. A small mineral water bottle was also placed on the desk, which she desperately gulped from, making the liquid inside her stomach rumble even more and her hunger pangs peak. As she was still looking around, her gaze fell on a man on the other side of the room, right across from her. Their eyes locked for a brief moment and she apologetically looked away, but the man made no attempt to shift his gaze. She felt his gaze on her, but Mansa didn't know how to handle it. She tried concentrating on the screen, but at intervals whenever she shifted angles, she felt her ears turning pink at his constant scrutiny.

When a waiter informed the presenter that coffee was served, he led them all to the far corner, where coffee and some modest refreshments were laid out. Mansa realized it was past 11 and she was famished. As luck would have it, the gentleman who had been sitting across from her handed over a plate to her, smiling graciously, causing her appetite to recede. Her hands began to perspire.

He was fair, of average height and had a lean frame. He wore a Rolex on his left wrist and had a regal air about him, a faint perfume clinging to him. The aroma of the snacks being served was camouflaged by a maze of fragrances emanating from all the attendees, who seemed to be outdoing each other with the brands they were sporting. Mansa felt lost for a moment. This, after all, was not where she belonged.

The warm touch of the plate and a gentle 'Hi' from the person beside her brought her back to her present surroundings. She greeted him back without smiling, but that didn't dissuade him from standing beside her to fill his plate. He did not say anything, but moved forward to sit at a table of four, where two ladies were already seated, engrossed in conversation. He gestured at Mansa to join them. He seemed to know the two women well. One was a dusky beauty and the other was a Kashmiri woman around Mansa's age. Both their faces lit up when they saw the man.

He suddenly extended his hand to Mansa and said, 'Hi! I am Pratap. Nice to meet you.' Mansa shyly took his hand before sitting.

The Kashmiri woman crisply introduced herself, 'I am Simran' and with a wink added, 'Newly single.'

The dusky one cocked her head in Mansa's direction in annoyance and said, 'You must be Mansa. I am Neena.'

Mansa realized that as she had reported late, her designated desk, which was closer to the presenter, had been hijacked by Neena, who was also a page three frequenter and a socialite. Neena didn't seem happy that Mansa had made it to class.

She didn't really want to lose her precious chair, which had such a good view of the AV screen. Simran, who herself had rosy cheeks, complimented Mansa on her hair and complexion.

To Mansa's chagrin, Neena chided Simran, 'You find every average-looking girl beautiful!' Her contempt for Mansa was quite obvious, making her feel uncomfortable.

Pratap cut in to defuse some of the tension, 'I'm glad that this course finally has an even number—a class of thirteen would be jinxed.' This didn't seem to lessen Neena's disdain for Mansa.

Mansa soon realized that they were all golfing buddies and ardent followers of Peter, a healer from Goa. The entire batch consisted of individuals who were followers of one guru or the other. It was unimaginable to them that somebody could look so fit and effervescent without ever having played a single sport. They found it harder to believe that Mansa was at peace with herself and not a follower of any guru or cult and liked it that way. Simran and Pratap then accompanied Mansa, introducing her to the rest of the coursemates as she had turned up late and missed the formal intro session.

A while later, a cheerful voice greeted her, 'Hey! I am Sapna.' Sapna appeared almost her own age. Another very sober and calm-looking woman who looked a few years younger stood behind Sapna. She introduced herself as Tushita, a journalist by profession and a Shambhala practitioner.

Mansa asked, 'Shambhala practitioner? What is that?' Tushita, with a calm smile told her it was an ancient Buddhist practice...'

Mansa smiled, thinking that people may come from diverse

professions and socio-economic backgrounds, yet they carried a common thread of being part of one religio-spiritual group or the other, usually the identities of their birth, the parents' religion most often becoming a child's faith. But the new fad, she had observed, was to follow alternate paths to faith and spirituality, not all of them validated.

She knew instantly that she was going to hit it off very well with Sapna and Tushita. After the break, they scurried back to their desks, as Gary Om, the venerable chef, was already standing in front of the AV screen. Neena dashed towards Mansa's desk, while Mansa nonchalantly occupied the place she had sat in earlier.

After spices and herbs, the lecture drifted towards the regions associated with those spices. Although Mansa was still not entirely sure that she belonged there, her participation in the group discussion and her knowledge on the subject gave her some confidence and had clearly impressed everyone present. Gary Om was so attuned with the group that time flew by swiftly when he spoke and soon it was 2.30 p.m. when everyone had to disperse.

As Mansa took the elevator down, a flurry of different thoughts flew through her mind—about the class, participants and so on. However, her foremost worry at the moment was how she would manage to get her car out if it were stuck between two cars. Parallel parking was her biggest challenge and her greatest pleasure when she successfully managed it. From a distance, she spotted her small car flanked by two swanky beauties, knowing that even grazing one of them while taking out her car would be sacrilegious. She walked hesitantly towards the parking lot, wondering if she could request a driver to help her out.

Soon enough, her eyes locked with Pratap in the back seat of a black Mercedes; his eyes were following Mansa intently. Sensing her dilemma, he sprang out and asked for her keys so she had no choice but to take his help. She flashed him a sincere smile of gratitude, as he got her car out for her from the tight space. Thanking him, Mansa was soon on her way home with a high she had never known before.

4

The World That Never Was

'Out of suffering have emerged the strongest souls; the
most massive characters are seared with scars.'
—Kahlil Gibran

MANSA FINALLY SEEMED to have found her calling in the new
cooking course that she had joined. Time seemed to flow rather
quickly now. And once the practical cooking classes began, the
course became even more interesting and the bond among the
attendees' also deepened. Mansa became less self-conscious and
became good friends with Pratap, Simran, Tushita and Sapna.

On Pratap's birthday, he had offered to take Gary and
some of the coursemates for an early evening coffee and cake
treat in a nearby restaurant. Once the lecture concluded, they
proceeded to the restaurant. Pratap had thoughtfully booked a
table so the six of them were seated without a fuss at a rather
prominent spot. Gary, Neena and Simran were familiar with

the restaurant, unlike Mansa, Sapna and Tushita who were first-timers. The simple charm of the place instantly made them comfortable. Once seated, the conversation flowed easily.

'Whenever I am in India, it is a must to have coffee here,' Gary admitted.

'I wonder why I haven't been here earlier,' Mansa had wondered aloud while Sapna and Tushita nodded their approval of the place.

Pratap, obviously, was very proud of his choice at this point. 'Ah! Because I was to have the privilege of introducing three beautiful ladies to this place,' he said with an affected air, and they all laughed together.

'What is it you were saying, Gary? Where do you live?' Sapna cut in.

'Well, I live in Singapore,' replied Gary, 'I own a restaurant chain there. My mother is an Indian, and our family enjoyed countless childhood vacations in Delhi, which has quite seamlessly made India my second home. Also, I tend to live out of a suitcase! Teaching the culinary art ensures I am busy lecturing in many parts of the world.' He went on to ask, 'What brought you all to this cooking class?'

Sighing deeply, Sapna told her story. 'I have two children, a seventeen-year-old daughter and a twelve-year-old son. I am doing pretty well for myself. I get lot of assignments from embassies, MNCs and the government. My husband owns a restaurant, but business has been rather dull for quite some time now. I really want to help him revive the place, it has so much potential. So, though I was firmly set in my line, my husband's worries impelled me to take this up.'

Pratap cheered Sapna, commending her strength and grit in the face of the odds. Somehow, Pratap getting comfortable with his new peers was not going down very well with Neena, and she blurted out, 'Sorry, guys, I will have to leave. I am expected at another party.' Simran tried convincing her to stay back, but her efforts were futile. Neena zoomed out before saying much and the conversation resumed again.

Sapna thought for a moment and said, 'My husband has filed for a divorce. I would grant him that, since we have grown apart, but my younger one is a special child and I can't deprive him of his father's love and attention. If I devote some time to the restaurant and it starts doing well then maybe it will restore his self-esteem and we can salvage our marriage.' Mansa wondered how she would have handled a similar situation and shuddered to even think of it. So that was the harsh, ugly truth—and still the woman was standing strong.

Simran felt sorry for Sapna and chimed in, 'Maybe and maybe not. But it is a chance well worth taking, Sapna.'

Everyone became thoughtful. They had all been together for over two weeks now, but Sapna had such a pleasant disposition that nobody could have guessed her pain.

Mansa thought, *we all carry such a complicated matrix of pain within us and the surface reveals so little.*

The waiter had arrived and was noting down their orders. The unanimous choice was falling on cool smoothies or hot chocolate, except for Sapna and Gary. Sapna ordered a wine and Gary a beer.

They all fixed their gaze on Tushita who hadn't spoken a word since they had arrived. Tushita smiled and said, 'Well,

I cover a gourmet food section for a major publication, and Gary Om is such a supreme chef and educator, I simply had to attend this course!'

Mansa remembered the word *Shambhala* and asked, 'Oh Tushita, please tell me something more about your spiritual side. I found your Shambhala practice introduction very intriguing.'

'I will take you to the ashram someday,' Tushita said with her characteristic calm.

Mansa's mind involuntarily drifted to Abhijit's recurrent nightmares, where no medication or counselling had helped. She said, impassioned suddenly, 'Somehow I am not very comfortable with this guru phenomenon that's become so pervasive. I don't know how and why I see a whole lot of gurus these days. Why can't we connect to our gods directly?'

'Why not, Mansa?' asked Pratap. 'Morality is at an all-time low. So I think these spiritual figures have a huge role to play.'

Mansa was in her element now. 'No, I don't think so. Although I have been brought up as a true-blue Hindu, of late at an objective level I do realize that if we handle religion emotionally then instead of being cohesive, it can be divisive.'

Simran and Sapna tried to lessen the seriousness of the discussion, 'Oh Mansa, it is Pratap's birthday—let's save the discussion for another day. Our drinks have arrived. Let's raise a toast to Pratap and our friendship.'

They all raised their glasses and mugs, grinning at the odd mix of clinks and thuds that resulted. After finishing their drinks and polishing off the cake, the group left the restaurant as it was already past 6 p.m.

Mansa quickly made for her car and on the way back home, found herself still admiring Sapna's courage. Mansa thought that the world outside her home was quite different, where people were bravely fighting their personal battles and still managed to be content and happy. In contrast, she had a struggle-free life but she had always felt something missing, a vacuum, but didn't quite know what. Mansa, secure at home under her husband's wings, had missed growing up in more ways than one. She had very little idea of the kinds of suffering and problems people encountered in their daily lives.

Although at a philosophical level, Mansa had always maintained that change and continuous evolution is the very essence of life and the moment you stop changing you decay, the changes she encountered when she stepped out were far too many than she had envisaged shut in the four walls of her home. She thought even after this limited exposure, she was in a better position to make observations from the point of view of a woman who made her home her whole world for twenty years.

She was observing a shift in the collective consciousness from religiosity to spirituality. Having grown up in a religious environment, she had internalized as a child that the essence of all religions was spirituality. Whether through rituals, idols or symbols, the quest is always to gear oneself towards the energy or pranik source of all consciousness, although some religions seemed to be more evolved than the others.

At one level, it seemed to be a refinement of the earlier religio-spirituality theory, yet at another level, she could not understand the trend galvanized by the media, especially the electronic media, creating larger-than-life gurus, who seemed to lay a new kind of trap for impressionable minds. Most of the people she came across seemed to be congregating around one guru or the other. She was beginning to understand that this pragmatism not only fulfilled their religio-spiritual needs, but also provided a social networking platform for occupational, professional, emotional, matrimonial and other needs.

From a distance, before the car entered the premises of their compound, she had spotted the tall frame of Abhijit in the veranda of their apartment floor. She looked up at him as she alighted and they both waved at each other.

As she entered the apartment, Abhijit and Bela both pounced on her with offers of tea. Mansa headed straight to Shonali's room after telling them, 'No thanks, too full today. Just had a large smoothie.'

Shonali looked up from her reading as her mother walked in, 'Mom, where have you been?'

Mansa chirped happily, 'It was a coursemate's birthday,' she told Shonali, 'and he took us all for a treat to a nearby restaurant. I really liked the place, you know. Next time when Malu is in town we must go there.' Shonali put her arms around her mother and Mansa mock-dragged her out of the room in the same hug to Abhijit.

Bela soon appeared with her usual request, 'Madam, could you please have your dinner a little early tonight as my favourite serial on TV will be on tonight.' Mansa although still feeling full and not in a mood to eat early due to the cake and smoothie still sitting in her stomach, always readily agreed to such requests.

As they settled early to bed, Mansa excitedly poured out

all the evening details of her newly made friends to Abhijit. She also told him about Simran's coming birthday next week.

'Abhi, would you mind if I went out with my gourmet group for a dinner next week for Simran's birthday?' she asked her husband.

Abhijit looking at her fondly as he said, 'Whatever makes you happy and you think is right is fine by me.'

Next morning as she reached her class, the first thing she did was accept Simran's birthday dinner invitation. Each one of them, including Neena, looked excited about Simran's coming birthday. Simran was in two minds, trying to decide whether she should have a small separate dinner for her gourmet class friends or invite them to the party she was throwing for her old friends. Finally, she decided on one big party.

Simran encouraged everyone to bring a partner so she invited Abhijit too. Mansa knew Abhijit would never come. As Gary entered the hall to lecture, the buzz stopped before Mansa had a chance to accept or decline on his behalf.

During the coffee break again the discussion took off.

'Guys, please suggest something,' said Simran. 'I am going crazy thinking about the venue and theme. Last night I was hanging out with my old buddies and we were up till late and couldn't decide. Now, come on show some spirit!'

Pratap grinned, 'A show of spirit you demand, ma'am? You mean only I can suggest a plan, not our dear delicate ladies?'

'Not a very clever joke, Pratap,' Simran said irritably, 'and please don't bug me right now. I have many things to do.'

'Let's go with a special colour,' suggested Neena.

'How about a wine-red or maroon? Maroon symbolizes

healing...' said Tushita.

Her idea clicked with everyone in the group, drawing ready acceptance. With maroon decided as the official colour of the party and the most chic pub as the venue for the party, Gary too had promised to join them.

In the evening, Abhijit's reaction was as Mansa had anticipated. He completely declined to join them, but also stated that Mansa must go. It left Mansa in dampened spirits again. She had never gone out at night without Abhjit but didn't feel like giving the party a miss either.

Next morning her friends at class could tell that something was amiss, since Mansa seemed sad. Towards the afternoon, Simran succeeded in getting Mansa's confession that she may not be able to join the party as her husband was not interested, surprising her friends. By the end of the day, everyone had got wind of the cause of her dilemma.

Pratap was exasperated, 'Come on, Mansa!' he exclaimed, 'Don't behave like a kid. You won't attend the party just because your husband is not coming? I think we are all over forty and responsible for how we act and what we do. If we can't take charge of our lives now, then when will we?'

Sapna and Tushita had also joined the conversation as they were all headed home. 'Mansa, it's about time in our lives that we should do what we like,' said Tushita.

Sapna too joined in, saying, 'Life is too short and who knows what will happen in the future? We all live once—so we should not suppress ourselves so much.'

'Although I don't agree with Sapna that we live only once, I do agree we should be true to ourselves and must do what brings us and others happiness. So there! It is decided that you are coming,' Tushita said firmly.

Mansa knew she had lost this battle, and since she so wanted to attend herself, she gave in willingly. When Pratap, however, suggested that he would ferry her to and fro, she politely declined saying she would be more comfortable with her driver.

With the matter finally decided, as she sat in her car, she asked the driver to go home via the mandir. It was a Monday ritual she had never missed since childhood. If she didn't find time in the morning then she always went to the temple in the evening. Under her grandmother's influence, she had always felt a special reverence for Lord Shiva.

On her way home she considered what gift to carry for Simran. The rest of the group were planning to carry different varieties of exotic wine. Mansa was in two minds as she had never gifted anyone alcohol before. She thought it would be best to discuss it with Abhijit.

The day of the party finally arrived and Mansa wore her prettiest maroon sari on Abhijit's advice. She had bought a trendy perfume wrapped in maroon paper as a gift though Abhijit had also suggested that wine would make a perfect birthday gift.

As she entered the pub she found herself in a room full of strangers. But very soon she was greeted with compliments by her new friends and felt comfortable at once. She sat at a table with Sapna and Tushita and was soon joined by Gary. In a couple of moments, Neena and Pratap arrived hand in hand too. They also joined the group. She again felt Neena's cold gaze scrutinizing her, but ignored her, relishing her snacks and a tall glass of mojito, for which she had developed a recent liking.

Loud music, sometimes classical and sometimes contemporary, both in Hindi and English rang out from the dance floor. The party was in full swing. Many people including Pratap and Neena had made it to the dance floor. Simran joined them and introduced them to a special friend, Vinod. Simran and Vinod appeared to be the co-hosts as they ensured that everyone was enjoying the party and then drifted to greet and mingle with the other guests. Soon Gary and Tushita also got up to dance. Sapna and Mansa smiled at each other, enjoying the music. Not up to dancing, they preferred chatting with each other.

Most people were on the dance floor. Laughter flew from all directions and suddenly a conversation from a nearby table caught her and Sapna's attention. Sapna smiled, touching her lips with her forefinger. She said softly, 'This is best pastime, eavesdropping and an interesting topic to overhear. Keep quiet, Mansa and listen.' Mansa turned to look at the adjoining table, where three men and a woman sat. They all seemed a little older than herself and Sapna.

The lady whom the men called Sri, was saying, 'Marriage as an institution has outlived its utility, yet we still stick to it. Any deviance from it is punishable by society and even puts a stigma on the women.'

The man called Chaddha said, 'You are right, Sri. It is not fair when people travel so much and meet new people all the time. It's no big deal to get attracted to another person after marriage.'

A male voice joined Sri in support saying, 'Totally, Sri.

Attraction to something new is the natural instinct of the human. When marriage came into being as an institution, the life expectancy was forty to fifty. Today people live up to ninety and spending over sixty years of life with the same person is not easy by any account. Now it was Sri's turn to stare at the man who had uttered this statement. The poor fellow was probably her husband for she screamed, 'Are you tired of me? Tell me?'

And the man, shocked at her outburst, cajoled her, 'But darling, I was only supporting your premise.'

Sapna and Mansa looked at each other and smiled at Sri's outburst. There was another person at the table who everyone referred to as Brigadier. He smirked and said, 'Sri, whether you like it or not, I dream that ten years from now I would want to settle in the Caribbean with a local beauty.' To this, Sri retorted sardonically, 'Yeah, I must share this good news with your wife Chandra first thing in the morning. By the way, why hasn't she come to the party?'

'You want me to be honest?' Brigadier parried. As Sri nodded, he went on, 'Believe it or not but when we are at home, Chandra says that she hates most of my friends and has had enough of them for over twenty-five years—she says that she cannot do it anymore! And she also says she would rather watch something on television, or read and then eat and sleep early than waste time with my friends.'

Mansa, who was listening attentively, thought this Chandra seemed so much like Abhijit. Maybe the only difference was that Chandra hated partying and had toed along with her husband for over twenty-five years before protesting and Mansa would have loved partying but had no opportunity to do so as Abhijit hated partying. Life is weird, she thought in her heart, wondering where was the harm in following what one likes to do sometimes.

Gary and Tushita were back at the table. Neena and Pratap were still dancing. Mansa looked at her watch and saw it was almost 9.30. *One-and-a-half hour had gone so quickly*, thought Mansa. She wanted to head for dinner soon after the birthday cake was cut although the rest of the gang were in the mood to stay on. Straight after the cake-cutting, Mansa went to fetch her dinner. Sapna, on seeing her uncertainty about staying back any further accompanied her for dinner, so that they could leave as soon as they finished eating.

Mansa and Sapna left while the party was still on. Sapna asked Mansa, 'Could you please drop me back home? I had to send the car for my children.' Mansa was only too happy for her company at this late hour of the night.

On their way back, Sapna complimented, Mansa, saying, 'It is so hard to guess your age. You are very lucky.'

Mansa smiled and saying thank you, asked, 'How old do you think Simran is?'

Sapna conjectured, 'I am not too certain but anything from thirty-six to forty-two'. And they both giggled together at their guesswork.

Mansa asked, 'Any idea what led to Simran's divorce? How long ago did it happen?'

Sapna said, 'Yeah actually, Neena told me. You know of course, that they are both very thick and golfing buddies.'

Mansa replied, 'Yes, of course I know.'

Sapna continued, 'According to Neena, Simran's in-laws were very propertied and influential people. Simran and her husband did not have a child even after over fourteen years of marriage. And there was pressure on her husband to divorce her and go in for a second marriage.'

Mansa was horrified, 'But that's illegal and even inhumane!' she exclaimed, aghast.

Sapna said, 'I guess a divorce was the only option left. She couldn't have stayed in a marriage where her honour and self-respect were threatened constantly by the idea of bringing another woman who would bear him a child. Good that she left him.'

Mansa agreed, 'Good she walked out.'

Sapna added, 'She recently got into a relationship with a college time sweetheart whom she wanted to marry. Her parents did not let her marry Vinod earlier because he was not as well off as Simran's family was. So today's party was special, a kind of celebration. Poor thing is so scared of marriage. Vinod wants to marry her, but Simran wants to wait.'

Mansa felt shaken. Even in this age of advancement some people only thought of women as objects of use and child-bearing machines that could be thrown out if found un-functional. Their wishes and aspirations had very little value when it came to prioritizing over a male family member, whether a sibling, a husband or a son. She thanked her stars for a caring and understanding husband.

After dropping off Sapna outside of her residence, as the car gained speed she was again thinking about the conversation she had just overheard. *It definitely had a point*, thought Mansa.

Mansa had been shocked and dismayed at people openly discussing their marriages and being part of extramarital relationships. But here they had seemed to be nice, responsible people, unlike the Bollywood villains she had thought them to be. She in principle agreed with what the Chaddha guy had said about a faster city pace and working lifestyle creating opportunities for men and women to be exposed to and interact with a greater number of likeminded people—meeting new people due to work, travel and wider experiences had brought about a polemical shift in the conventional definition of dating. 'Middle-age dating' was on its way to becoming a far common and accepted fact of life than it had ever been. She wondered to herself, were Pratap and Neena dating too? Or was it just a platonic interest? Maybe she should ask Sapna or Tushita next time. Thinking of Tushita, who had stayed single by choice and then Simran and Sapna's marital upheavals, she realized that the tribe of single, divorced, successful and socially acceptable women was growing.

Distances in Delhi, ever-speeding traffic and the lengthy queues at the Gurgaon Toll always gave her ample time to observe and reflect on the lives of the dwellers of this bustling megacity. She reasoned that first, the T.V. soaps had entered the drawing room and the subconscious of the Indian middle class, and now the social networking sites had attacked the Indian morality and mind with every networking giant strategizing to get as big a share as possible.

Separation and divorce were becoming more common. Many women appeared happily emancipated and dignified and even reasonable in their decision to walk out. But what dismayed and disgusted Mansa the most was the fact that morality in Indian marriages had gone for a toss as people cast their role models from the diet they were being served on their televisions on a daily basis. The most popular television soaps ran for a couple of years at least. To stabilize their TRP's, in their overstretched plots the soaps had devised an easy formula/ USP to retain the audience interest –romantically pairing every character of the soap with each other, and almost invariably a child before the wedlock appearing in some episode from most of the characters of the soap. Gullible viewers across the nation where 65 per cent humanity lives in rural India assuming this is what city life is. And in their bid to urbanize and modernize the youth forming their role models from the audio visual medium of daily soaps. She wondered why the human psyche is always attracted to negative things first.

A jerk from the car brakes brought her out of her thoughts. From a distance she noted Abhijit's tall figure pacing in the veranda waiting for her. A tad guilty, she waited for the driver, Sanjay, to park and lock the car. She quickly collected the car keys and ran for the steps as fast as she could. As she reached the apartment, she was accosted by Abhijit, 'How was the party? It's almost 11 and I was worried sick for you.'

'Why should you worry? Am I a child? Do I look irresponsible on any count?' Mansa jumped to her defence and walked off to change after her retort which was becoming so very frequent these days.

Abhijit tried to mollify her, 'That's not what I meant at all, Mansa. You know it how unsafe Delhi is … and especially Gurgaon.'

Something in Mansa had snapped by now. She couldn't put her finger on it but she felt suffocated. She couldn't hold back her irritation even an iota. Seething, she said, 'DON'T worry about me. I had decent company … as it is, half my mind was on you. I could have enjoyed the party so much better if you were not such a nervous type!' She sprawled on the bed, pulling the cover on herself from toe to head and slept, leaving Abhijit befuddled.

The days at the cookery classes were Mansa's new lease on life. Gradually, Mansa's confidence was growing as she knew she was picking up well and a few sincere offers of help from Gary and Pratap, among others, gave a new boost to her confidence.

Gary arranged for the batch to join an internship programme with a famous international restaurant chain. Going out from her home, working and meeting people, was giving her thrills she had never known before. She wondered if the changes she had felt in her psyche were a reflection of the social transformation that the society as a whole was going through or something else within her was changing. Or were they the bottled emotions of an incomplete youth that were now emerging? Sometimes she thought that she had been a good daughter, sister, wife, mother, daughter and daughter-in-law, but where was *she* in this multiplicity of roles? Had she been fair to herself? When and where did her youth go?

She had only partially savoured the compliments from her new friends Sapna, Tushita and Simran who had said that the naivety, ignorance and innocence she carried within were probably why she looked years younger than her actual age. She remembered how in school sometimes friends had teased her for her naivety and her eyes welled up. With a new determination, she thought she must change her life to prove to herself that she could grow, lifting herself from the cocoon she had existed in.

Six weeks just flew and she was excitedly looking forward to her first day of internship arranged by Gary with a five-star hotel. As she reported for work on her first day she was sent for a briefing and orientation to the senior manager, Mr Sethi's, office. He was a perfect gentleman and took her around for a tour of the entire hotel, trying to educate her not only on the culinary aspect of hospitality but also introducing her to the healthy relationship between perfect housekeeping, hospitality and food. As he elucidated on many new aspects on the tour, her enthusiasm and energy knew no bounds. She was determined to work as hard as she could.

As the tour drew to its end, Mansa said fervently, 'Thank you, sir, thank you so much. It was so informative.'

Mr Sethi, replied, 'Oh! You are most welcome, sweetheart.'

Sweetheart? Looking down at her modest sari, she wondered if something was wrong with the way she had dressed or if this was how men addressed women these days. She had no clue. However, she couldn't deny the fact that she was enjoying the attention of male and female colleagues alike and was pleased to be popular in her new circle in the hospitality industry. Many men she met these days, at the gym or at work also tried to get to know her better, asking her out for tea or coffee. She hadn't realized so far that 'middle-age dating', had become this common. She even found it difficult to come to terms with the idea of having a working lunch or dinner with a male colleague outside of office. Painstakingly and with a healthy dose of curiosity, she began her new journey in the world of wine tasting and gourmet bites. Being a teetotaller, it wasn't easy for her to experiment with and relish wines, but the food part came effortlessly to her, as she had a natural sense of spices and seasonings. She was enjoying her journey into the culinary world so far and wondered what life would have in store for her in the future.

5

Happy Days are Here Again

'The wound is the place where the Light enters you.'
—Rumi

THIS WAS THE beginning of a happy phase in Mansa's life. It was a happiness that came from an awareness of herself, something she had not experienced in a long time or perhaps ever. The last time she had felt awash in this kind of thrill was during college, but she had been too timid and cowardly even to admit to herself that she had enjoyed the attention of the opposite sex and back then, she was so moralistic that she felt it was a taboo, something good girls did not indulge in. As a result, she had met all the attention from young suitors with contempt. So now, she failed to understand why she felt so thrilled and good about herself when Pratap and other colleagues, male and female, showered their attention on her.

She felt so spirited the entire day that in the evening when she reached home before Abhijit, she paced the veranda to welcome him, share her excitement and give him an account of the day's happenings. Abhijit seemed to delight in her happiness.

Seeing her bubbly after a long while, Abhijit said, 'Mana, let's have some tea together.' Abhijit had addressed her lovingly with this moniker after a long time. Although Mansa wanted to have tea in the veranda, she gave in to Abhijit's love for stretching his legs on the bed in the evening with a tray of tea perched beside them, along with his favourite Indian sweets: laddu and gulab jamun. The entire household reverberated with their jokes and laughter. Shonali quietly came in and tucked herself beside her mom. She was a sensitive child and very proud of her mother.

It had been years since Mansa had waited for a new morning so excitedly. She was up unusually early and was done with tea by 6.30 a.m. Absently, she stared at the table clock, contemplating whether to go to the gym or not, as she didn't want to be late during her internship period. She hurriedly jumped out of the bed, deciding in favour of a short, quick six-kilometre run instead of the gym, so that she could be back by 7.30. She dashed towards the bathroom to quickly grab her hanging track suit. Once ready, she threw a quick glance in Abhijit's direction, asking if he would join her. Over the years, she had become so used to him declining to join her in any social activity, recreational or otherwise, that it had even stopped hurting. She realized now that unknowingly, Abhijit's lack of interest in an active social life and her dull days and boring evenings were alienating them from each other. However, there were few arguments and interactions, as Abhijit never lost his temper, even at the worst provocation. Compliments, such as 'best bahu' and 'great wife' from her friends and relatives only irritated her now. She wondered if this was what people called a mid-life crisis.

She thanked her stars that at least she had started giving a purpose to her life albeit so little and so late. Now, she had started going out with her new friends in the evenings and deeply regretted the lost two decades of her life. How much had she missed on the social front and why? She had gone to great lengths to flash big smiles and not showed how disappointed she felt with her husband's perennial refusals to join her for a morning jog or for that matter any recreational, sporty or distantly romantic activity. Today, it didn't matter. She flashed a smile at his sleepy back and quickly went out.

Mansa had slipped into a new kind of morning rhythm. She enjoyed dressing up every morning. Her computer skills had improved and she could type at a slow pace, but was still largely dependent on Shonali for her email and internet-related activities.

Six months of internship passed very quickly. She made many important contacts and picked up the subject very fast. Mansa made another small beginning from home soon after interning. On Pratap's suggestion, she started a website on healthy, nutritive gourmet bites, which she named Abhimansa. Many of her coursemates—Tushita, Sapna, Simran and even Neena had promised to help and support her. Mr Sethi and many colleagues she got to know during her internship programme were extremely helpful and encouraging. They gave her many practical tips on setting up a small enterprise from home. She started customizing and designing party menus, which not only looked attractive on a platter, but were also nutritious. She was slowly becoming popular for her innovative recipes and menus. Her kitchen soon became a recipe laboratory. Her love for cooking, which had been suppressed so far, had resurfaced and taken on another dimension.

The response was so positive that within two years she was able to employ a food technologist, a dietician and some support staff as part of her initial team and was ready to move to a modest office of her own. She was at last on the way to fulfilment.

Mansa felt very lucky to be completely supported by Abhjit and Shonali emotionally. She realized that the hours spent outside of her home were constantly increasing. Success was coming but not without a cost because it coincided with her period of struggle with Shonali.

When it was still early days for Mansa in her new business, Shonali's constantly deteriorating school performance was an indicator that her mother's involvement in Shonali's academics had come to a bare minimum. Shonali's poor pre-board result was worrying and Mansa's consternation had been on a rise since the morning.

She was in the process of setting up her newly rented office and pressures of time-bound deliverables were mounting too. Radhika, her faithful assistant, had been with her round the clock, right from negotiating the rent to practically setting up every bit in their new office.

Only last week, when she had hurried home earlier than

usual to check on Shonali's preparation for the exam, she had faced a major shock.

When she came home around 4 p.m., Shonali's room was closed from inside. Bela was enjoying her afternoon siesta and Abhijit was in office. She felt a bit odd. Why should Shonali's room be closed from inside when there was no noise at home to disturb her? She knocked, guessing angrily.

'Shona...Shonali...what are you up to? Open the door.' She knocked again violently. 'Open the door, I say!'

It was quite a few moments before the door was opened. Her motherly sensors completely on and seething with anger, she pleaded, 'Shona...what are you up to? Television? Don't you want admission in any university? Who do you think you are? Some billionaire's daughter? You actually think money grows on trees?'

'Just fifteen minutes back, I called you on the way and you said you were writing a timed mock test. Since when have you learnt to lie? I knew... I just knew something else was up your sleeve and see how right I am!'

Violently, she charged towards Shonali's almirah. 'I know it's not the television alone. Today I am going to set you just right. Wait.'

Shonali pleaded, shielding her almirah, 'Mom... Mom... please... I promise it won't happen again. Please, one last chance, I promise. One last time.'

Mansa had kept charging, pushing Shonali aside. She didn't have to work too hard to retrieve the x-box which she had confiscated at once. She slapped Shonali hard and then was violently shaking and helplessly crying, repenting her excessive action. She sank on the edge of the bed, weeping. 'I am really sorry... I shouldn't have let you make me so angry. How much you promised in the morning that you would stay away from TV and the x-box till your tenth standard board exams get over. I should never have worked. I am to be blamed. No work from now on. I will sit at home from tomorrow. You can't do without a guard, I can see.'

Shonali had completely broken down with guilt. 'No, Mom! I promise to be more responsible. You have already done enough for our home. You enjoy your work so much. Don't even think like that. I promise. I truly promise I'll study hard.'

They had sat hand in hand for a long time, Mansa still consumed with shame at losing her temper, especially when she thought that it was her fault to be away at such a crucial point in time for her daughter.

6

The Magic Weaver

'I love you as certain dark things are to be loved, in secret, between the shadow and the soul.'

—Pablo Neruda

On a pleasant April night, in 2012, Mansa was preparing to go to bed. Abhijit appeared to be fast asleep, earlier than usual, and she could not hear Shonali stirring in her room either. She got up, zombie-like, to peep inside Shonali's room before heading to her bathroom. Washing her feet under a quick stream of water was a ritual Mansa couldn't do without before going to sleep, which was followed by brushing her teeth, washing her face and applying night cream. The time was almost 10 p.m. Bela was also done winding up the kitchen.

While she washed her feet under the warm stream of water, Mansa's thoughts ran amok. *Though we all live together in small or large families as a part of societies, cities, states and nationalities, each one of us carries a vacuum or an inner world of our own within ourselves, which we allow people in only when we really want to. No one outside can peep into that void. All of us have two selves. One is who we actually are and the other is how we want to be seen by others,* she thought.

As Mansa came out of the bathroom, she saw Bela placing her glass of milk on her side table and arranging her water tray for the night. 'Madam, your hot milk is kept on the bedside table. Please don't forget to drink it. Do you want anything else? Should I put out the veranda lights?'

Mansa nodded lightly while drying her feet on a white towel. As she moisturized them, her gaze went to the window opposite her bed. The garden outside was bathed in a phenomenal play of darkness and light with fireflies shining brightly. A stunning starry night was made further resplendent by a three-fourths full moon.

Although it was the beginning of April, Mansa still needed her stole to wrap around her when the air-conditioner was on. She sat up on her bed, stretching her legs out. She rested her back against the bed rest, making herself comfortable and began sipping her milk slowly, reflecting upon her day.

A book lay open, half-read, on her side of the bed. Besides the water tray, the table held a huge stack of books piled on top of one another, an alarm clock and some tall bottles with her potions. The room had mostly bare walls. On one side of the bed hung some of hers and Abhijit's portraits along with their wedding photograph. The wall behind the bed was adorned with pictures of her sisters, daughters and a single frame of her late parents.

She browsed her social networking site for a few minutes and read for a while before finally retiring for the day. She had just attended a college alumni meet a couple of days ago. Friend requests from people she had met at the college alumni meet hadn't ceased coming in yet. Many people had attended it, and for those abroad who couldn't attend, photographs had been uploaded on the college's official alumni page. So Mansa had befriended many of her classmates once again after decades. She had also accepted friend requests from others whom she hadn't met personally, but who had been in either of her sisters' batches. She had always refused to accept requests from people she had not met, but she felt that it would be rude to not accept requests from people point blank.

As she was browsing, she received a request from someone, whose profile appeared to be different from the rest. Strangely, the name—Rajan Chopra—rang an instant bell in her mind and seemed vaguely familiar. The request had come accompanied with a swish of poetry, which completely floored her.

Mansa wondered why she felt that the name was vaguely familiar. She had never experienced this kind of feeling before. She saw that he was from Meera's batch, but she had not heard about him from Meera ever. More than anything else, she felt an inner pull, which made her immediately accept his request. As soon as she had accepted his request, bang came poem after poem in her personal message inbox in English, Hindi and Persian. Quotes from movies and classics soaked in romance followed.

It all perplexed Mansa a great deal, but the avalanche of poetry and romantic quotes left her with no time to react sternly in her characteristic manner. At first, she just laughed it off, but for some mysterious reason, she wanted to go on reading whatever came her way.

As evident from his limited profile, Rajan Chopra seemed to be a suave, successful entrepreneur from London Business School, who was currently settled in Los Angeles with his family. From his profile, he seemed like quite a lady's man, capable of quoting romantic and philosophical poetry and discussing sovereign ratings or any other diverse topic under the sun. However, there were no photographs of him.

Soon she felt he was trying too hard to impress her with his posts and private messages, but felt flattered nonetheless. With as intelligent and bright a companion as Abhijit, she had never come across anyone else who had been able to impress her. She was the sort of person who was impossible to please, leave aside impress. Even before Abhijit had entered her life, she had never been easily awed or carried away by flattery. And with Abhijit in her life, the bar had been raised to an unscaleable height.

After Rajan had finished his poetic discourse, he started a conversation with her.

Rajan: *Thanks for accepting my request. Welcome to my world.*

Mansa: *So you are from my sister's class. Did we meet in college? I don't recall ever meeting you.*

Rajan: *I am sure we didn't. Would never have forgotten you...*

Mansa: *Why...What's so special about me?*

Rajan: *So, quite a few of you met at the alumni meet.*

Mansa: *Were you there? Did we see each other?*

Rajan: *Nope, I am miles away.*

Mansa: *Miles away? Where?*

Rajan: *West Coast, Los Angeles—the most happening and beautiful city in the world, just like you.*

Mansa: *Excuse me, what do you mean just like me?*

Rajan: *I left home soon after the twelfth. And it's been a long journey since.*

Mansa was slightly annoyed that he had avoided her questions twice, but was greatly intrigued by him and typed: *Tell me your story.*

After a long silence, Rajan replied: *It's just that we are always trying to do our best in so many spheres and once, I took the road less travelled. Like Robert Frost said:*

> *I shall be telling this with a sigh*
> *Somewhere ages and ages hence:*
> *Two roads diverged in a wood, and I—*
> *I took the one less travelled by,*
> *And that has made all the difference.*

After a pause, he wrote: *What about you?*

Mansa: *Everyone's life doesn't traverse the same path.*

Somewhere in her tender and melancholy heart, the lines touched a deep chord. She could almost experience the latent anguish and pain in those lines and her heart melted. Perhaps the deep solitude within and the dark night outside also played the trick. Something in the lines resonated with her—she had once chosen a path without much ado. Not that she had ever regretted that choice, but it had made her life predictably comfortable and had prevented her from experiencing and exploring life.

Mansa at first felt inexplicably drawn to Rajan despite her reservations. But soon, after a few more messages over a couple of days, she was enchanted and captivated by the poetry and his conversations, completely carried away by his charm. She felt attracted towards him, and thought, *here is a self-made character, who has gone through many lows and highs of life. He seems to have worked his way up to achieve what he has.* She felt that he had not accepted life on a platter the way she had.

She started warming up to the stranger in a most uncharacteristic manner. She saw an unseen ally in him, someone she could share even the vaguest or deepest of her thoughts with without being judged. Although she could never fully fathom what was going on in his mind, she began to trust him blindly. Rajan's light romantic tone and unique style of messaging stirred many complex emotions in her which she had never experienced before.

Strangely, over the next few days whenever she was online, he appeared online too. She felt conscious of his presence and always waited for him to begin the conversation.

Like any other night, she was online, subconsciously waiting for Rajan to begin.

Rajan: *Hi*

Mansa: *Hi*

Rajan: *What did you say about yourself last night? I didn't get any sleep and revisited our entire conversation.*

Mansa: *Oh, I am really sorry. I never meant to disturb you.*

Rajan: *Well, don't overestimate yourself, you are not disturbing me.*

Mansa: *Oh my God! You have such a huge ego, your LBS ego.*

Rajan: *What makes you say that? I can even laugh at myself. Few can.*

Mansa remained silent, not sure what to say. Rajan resumed the conversation after a few minutes.

Rajan: *Sari, churidar, dresses! You ladies do some wonderful work.*

Mansa marvelled at the ease with which he conversed with her and to her disbelief uttered: *Are you checking out my profile?*

Without bothering to answer her, he continued: *Sari! Sari it is. You look great in a sari!*

Mansa blushed and feeling elated, typed: *I am flattered. Thanks.*

She went back to his profile out of curiosity. Barring education and career, it had very limited information and hardly any pictures. It didn't say whether he was single or married. The profile picture displayed a little boy, who she presumed could be his son. But somewhere her brain censors also warned her to be careful since she couldn't be sure who he really was. The boy looked about one to two years old. As she scrolled through his profile, she found photographs of various sports, some famous pieces of poetry, and a list of city marathons. Her eyes lit up.

She typed as fast as she could: *I also participated in a half marathon last year.*

Rajan: *Oh, you are my guru then.*

Mansa: *I want to tell you something about my marathon.*

Rajan: *I want to tell you something about saris.*

Mansa was taken aback by his statement. Her heart skipped a beat; no one had ever spoken to her in such a flippant, flirty manner. Uncharacteristically, she turned pink, amused and spellbound. She experienced a heady mix of fear, curiosity and excitement. Some involuntary muscle in her body made her upload a profile photograph of hers in a sari instantly.

Rajan: *Why did you do that?*

Mansa did not have any answer to that question.

Rajan: *Tell me why you did that.*

Mansa did not know what to say and he kept repeating his question.

She suddenly turned stiff, her heart thumping loudly. She wondered if the faraway stranger could peep at the rush of emotions within her heart. She felt unsteady. She had been unprepared for his kind of wit and unconventional expression, and her body's response to it. Her alchemy triggered unknown reactions in her system. She had not known this kind of pleasure from talking before, and was suddenly aware of every fragment in her body.

Mansa: *Did you know my sister, Meera, well in college?*

Rajan: *Had I known she had a pretty sister like you, I would definitely have made more of an effort to know her.*

Mansa: *That's hardly an answer to my question.*

Rajan: *Well! I was in your sister's class for only one year.*

He seemed disinterested in taking the topic further and Mansa did not press him.

Rajan: *Tell me, why did you upload that picture of yours in a sari?*

Mansa did not answer and felt extremely embarrassed at what she had done.

Rajan: *Okay, tell me, what is your occupation?*

Mansa: *I started working very recently just about couple of years back. Hubby wanted me home with children when they were growing up so there was hardly any opportunity to work.*

Rajan: *It's not nice to stop someone from working.*

Mansa: *No, it was in the best interest of the family at that time. Hubby is a gentle and very accomplished person.*

Rajan: *I wish we had met in school. How perfect it would have been*

You and me, me and you, in school; a girl and a boy, and a boy and a girl.

Mansa smiled and typed: *Well… we didn't.*

He suddenly popped a question: *If I were to come to India, would you take me out for lunch?*

At first, she wasn't sure how to react. As conservative as she was, too shy in her younger days to even converse with the opposite sex, this time she couldn't react with a sharp no; instead, she saw herself type softly: *Who knows if I will be in Delhi when you come here.*

She wanted to ask how often he came to India, but couldn't. Yet again, they were so absorbed in talking that they lost track of time. It was Robert Frost sometimes, Ghalib, then Faiz Ahmed Faiz, Jigar, Firaq, and several other greats, whose names she had only heard. To Mansa, the world around her ceased to exist and time seemed to have stopped. She was only conscious of Rajan. That night, they finally bid each other goodbye at around 2 a.m.

Abhijit had turned a few times in her direction to see what was going on, but he was not the pushy or suspicious kind. He had simply asked, 'Mansa, what keeps you awake so late?'

Mansa, unsure about what to say, blurted out, 'I am practising online to improve my skills. You know how I need to upgrade them to handle my work efficiently. I am not even thorough with MS Word yet. If it's disturbing your sleep, I can practise somewhere else for a while.'

Abhijit had simply gone back to sleep without even bothering to answer her and Mansa had carried on. Even after ending the chat, that night she had lain awake, happily wrapped in Rajan's thoughts. For the first time in her life, she had no control over her emotions, no logic or self-control seemed to be working. She felt very feminine. It felt wonderful to be admired by someone, to know that someone was trying hard to impress her with poetry and romance, both of which were new to her.

It became a routine for her—as soon as she reached her office, her hands would reach out straight for her laptop in an obsessed manner and constantly keep refreshing the page. As he lived in Los Angeles and she in New Delhi, he was exactly twelve-and-a-half hours behind India time. Her morning office hours, when work pressure was the lightest and she was away from the routine responsibilities of home, perfectly synchronized with his bedtime.

Once, she found a Persian couplet waiting in her message box 'اری شُقنِ مدق بید یبیبخ'

She stared at it, completely clueless about the script and what it meant. At long last, the green dot on the chat window appeared and Rajan was online. Mansa asked him to explain the meaning of the couplet, since she did not understand any

Persian. Rajan was happy to oblige.

Rajan: *It means, wherever I look, my eyes see only your reflection and see nothing besides you.*

Mansa: *Ahaa, really? It's so flattering. Are you trying to make fun of me? Are you laughing? Who are you with?*

Rajan: *Oh, come on. There is no one. It's just me and my one-year-old son. I am trying to put him to sleep.*

Mansa: *How do I know that you are by yourself and not a couple of friends just trying to bully someone online?*

Rajan: *Well, you've got to trust me.*

Mansa: *You are trying to put your son to sleep?*

Rajan: *Yeah, I put him to sleep every night.*

Mansa felt a rush of instant sympathy and affection, dispelling all her fears about him. She wondered what could have led to a man being all alone, trying to put his one-year-old child to sleep at this unearthly hour. What kind of a wife would allow that? No wonder he sought someone to talk to. She felt like filling his emptiness with her own deep void. She thought to herself that it wasn't exactly wrong if two lonely people have a pleasant exchange of thoughts.

Mansa: *At times I feel very lonely too.*

Rajan: *I don't feel lonely. I enjoy my solitude and especially talking to you.*

He sent another couplet her way:

Ab hai khushi khushi mein na gham hai malaal mei
Duniya se kho gaya hoon tumhaare khayaal mein

(No pleasure in happiness I feel, nor pain in any suffering

So lost in your thoughts am I, that I am lost to the
world)

Although floored, Mansa once again did not know what
to say. He seemed to possess a repertoire of poetry perfect
for every situation, which immensely impressed and charmed
her. She read the poetry and was touched by the words. She
forgot that Rajan was probably waiting for a response. Soon,
he messaged again.

Rajan: *Don't you like talking to me?*

Feeling awkward, Mansa was at a loss of words. With great
difficulty she managed to type: *Hmm.*

Rajan: *What, hmm? You like it or you don't?*

Her heartbeat quickened with the question.

To distract him, she asked: *Where did you learn such good
Persian? I am so impressed, seems unusual for a person of your
profile to know so much poetry and such fine Persian.*

Rajan: *I was brought up in a house where people heard and
appreciated all kinds of poetry, especially Persian; so it came
naturally to me.*

Mansa: *Hmm, I am so impressed.*

Then she quickly typed: *I better get back to my work. Bye.*

Rajan: *No wait. I want to add you somewhere.*

Mansa: *Where?*

Rajan: *I have added you. It's my group, and of some of my
very own people. It's a very personal and special group.*

Feeling very special, Mansa thanked him and began browsing
through the group. She found that the group comprised a
number of men and women. From the profile pictures, she saw

many were very chic women. She found some familiar names from her college too. She could make out how popular he was with the women. She had left poetry and ghazals somewhere behind in her life, and felt very charmed and fascinated by the interesting posts in the group. He immediately posted some romantic couplets in the group while they were chatting.

shaam-e-gum kuchh us nigaah-e-naaz ki baatein karo bekhudi ba.
Dhatii chali hai raaz ki baatein karo
nakhat-e-zulf-e-pareshaan,
daastaan-e-shaam-e-gum subah hone tak isi andaaz ki baatein karo
kuchh qafas ki tiliyon se chhan rahaa hai nuur saa kuchh fazaa kuchh hasarat-e-paravaaz ki baatein karo

(It is an evening of sadness, talk to me of those luminous eyes
Intoxication is yet growing, talk to me of secrets
Fragrance of your dishevelled hair, story of this sad evening
Talk to me of such things till dawn breaks
Sieving through bars of my cage, some soft radiant light
Talk to me some of spring, and some of my desire to fly away)

Although instantaneously, many of his female friends started commenting on and liking the ghazal, Mansa knew that it was only for her. Even though she only partially understood its meaning, she turned crimson, as though everyone in the group knew that it was to welcome her. Self-consciously she bid him goodbye. Returning to office work was not easy with thoughts of him continuously knocking at the doors of her mind.

It was a typical office morning and it was imperative to hold the usual 10 a.m. meeting. Mansa herself had laid down the firm rule but ever since Rajan had entered her life, the rule had more or less been overlooked. In the evening a major deliverable was due to the German embassy. The embassy had requested Abhimansa for some authentic Bavarian dishes for a Europian delegation of 50 people with diverse food preferences. As Abhimansa's focus and forte was vegetarian, she always had to delegate the non-vegetarian part of the cuisine to one of her friends' boutique restaurants. She usually relied on one of Pratap's restaurants for this. But some of the past orders had been well taken care of by Sapna's restaurant, which had somewhat picked up.

She called a meeting in her chamber to decide all the modalities of the evening in detail. She constantly looked at her watch, anxiously thinking that if the meeting continued, Rajan may fall asleep without talking to her. The thought was so unbearably unpleasant that when they broke for coffee at 12 during the meeting, she had half a mind to turn her office colleagues from her room to the common area to steal a few words with him. Somehow with great difficulty, she controlled herself but she knew that everyone had noticed her lack of interest in work. She was scared that not only would they lose an important client if the order was not executed well, but their reputation too would be at stake in the embassy circuit. Finally, when all ends were taken care of around 2 p.m.

everyone left her room and she leapt at her laptop. He was not there, leaving her with a feeling of desolation.

Even while following her busiest and most challenging office routine, he was always present in some corner of her mind. She enjoyed being left alone and thinking of only him. It was as though a torrential rain shower had suddenly flooded a desiccated river. The days seemed longer than usual, as at the back of her mind she waited for the hour when she could reconnect with the stranger. She was always in an unusual hurry to wind up her evening chores. Even while she ate her favourite Chinese meal with Abhijit and Shonali, her mind kept wandering, thinking about what he would be doing at that moment.

One night, she did not even make her customary post-dinner round to the veranda overlooking the golf course and headed straight to the bathroom to complete her cleansing ritual. She wanted to catch up with Rajan as early as possible. She landed in bed well before 10 p.m., which was her usual bedtime.

As always at that time, he was there when Mansa logged in. Both waited for a while for the other to begin the conversation. Finally, when Mansa couldn't wait any longer she typed: *Hi!*

Rajan: *I was wondering if you would say hi at all.*

Mansa: *Why wouldn't I?*

Ignoring her question, in his usual style, Rajan spouted some more couplets and suddenly said: *My wife even forgot our anniversary this year.*

Mansa felt greatly pained when she read that. She typed: *How long have you been married?*

Rajan: *Eight years.*

Mansa: *Oh, I am really feeling bad for you. So that's why you talk to me?*

Rajan: *Oh, no. You are you. I like you. Enjoy talking to you. It's just that we were relocating. A one-year-old and we were tired and overworked and hadn't slept well.*

Mansa: *Hmm.*

The respect and soft corner for him in her heart widened.

Rajan: *And you?*

Mansa: *I have been married for a long time, really long. It feels like I was born married over twenty years while I was still studying. My elder daughter is studying dentistry in UK and the younger one will finish school in two years.*

Rajan: *Why is it that you mostly talk in monosyllables and why is it always me who says hi first?*

Mansa: *Not true... but I am a very shy person and you are the first guy I have opened up to so much and chatted with. I don't think it's a good idea to talk to strangers much. I hardly know you. I only know my husband and some cousins, as I started working just a couple of years back. So, besides the kitty ladies, I never had an opportunity to meet other people. It's only recently that my social circle has expanded due to my work commitments. I still struggle with the computer at times though.*

Rajan: *Well, you have to trust me. As Jason Fraz sang,*

Open up your mind and see like me. Open up your plans and damn, you're free. Look into your heart and you'll find that the sky is yours. So please don't, please don't, please don't...

There's no need to complicate. 'Cause our time is short.
This oh, this oh, this is our fate. I'm yours.

They both remained silent for a while. She experienced a unique connection with him in those moments of silence and her mind vouched that he was her quintessential lost hero of many lives.

Then suddenly, waking up to the implications of what he was saying, Mansa instantly logged out without saying another word. She lay down on her side, her heart beating loudly once again, her female hormonal rush surging the way it never had before. She was definitely enjoying his attention and did not want to lose him. Whenever he typed, 'I'm yours', it had such an electrifying effect on her.

But she also knew that no matter what, if he crossed a line or messed with her sensibilities, she would have no choice but to delete or block him. She prayed, 'Oh God, please let him be a decent person! I so enjoy talking to him. Please Bhagwan, let my misgivings that he might be a womanizer be false.'

She wondered yet again why she was getting so interested in another man and enjoying it so much. Long ago, during the internet boom in India, her friends had told her that many people stayed glued to chatting at the cost of their work, marriage and family, and that there were special websites that offered X-rated content. Many men befriended women online to have a good time. She had even seen a close friend's marriage go through many ups and downs as a result of her husband's addiction to the cyber world. Mansa heard herself pray that Rajan would not be one of those cyber-sex maniacs and would not do anything to hurt her sentiments.

She turned to look for Abhijit, but he hadn't joined her in bed yet. She shut her eyes, trying to conjure up a picture of Rajan in her mind. Soon after, she felt Abhijit's hand gently nudging her waist. Although awake, she didn't turn in his direction, pretending to be asleep. And soon she heard his snores.

Everything was the same—the same house, golf course view, day and night—but Mansa found everything transformed, more meaningful and cheerful. Suddenly, life didn't seem all that boring, dull and routine-bound. With Rajan around, life seemed to be worth living.

Next day, she thought about Shonali, who had been urging her to take her to the Mall ever since her board exams had got over. In the evening, she decided to give Shonali a surprise by winding up her work a little early and landing up straight at the tennis court to pick her up for shopping. The moment Shonali saw her coming in, she chirped, 'Oh, Mom you are here...'

'Yup, let's go...your shopping was due...right?'

Shonali excitedly hugged her, 'Oh, Mom... I really love you! Let's go.'

'Where would my princess like to go?' Mansa asked.

'DLF Promenade!' was the instant excited squeal

Mansa asked Sanjay to take the car to the mall. Once they were inside the mall, Shonali was a ball of extreme excitement. And Mansa wondered whether she had neglected Shonali under the burden of her growing work. She promised herself she would make up for all the lost time. Mother and daughter enjoyed some frozen yogurt and then went to Shonali's favourite clothing stores.

Mansa curiously strolled from one object to the other,

she opened the chat box. Soon, she heard the familiar ping on laptop.

Rajan: *Hi*

Mansa paused, wondering whether she should reply or not, as suddenly she felt self-conscious about talking too much with a stranger and getting carried away with his charming words, and the fact that she loved every moment of it. Finally, when she couldn't control the temptation, she replied: *Hi.*

There was a long silence on both sides. Mansa's heart kept somersaulting. Finally, Rajan broke the silence.

Rajan: *I keep thinking of your beautiful eyes. Do you ever think of me?*

Mansa knew that she could not answer his question truthfully, as he was constantly in her thoughts, so she kept quiet, ignoring the question.

Rajan: *You have a nice name. I love your name, Mansa... oh, I just love your name.*

Reading the lines almost caused Mansa to stop breathing. She retorted: *There is nothing special about this name. I hate my name. Your name is so much better.*

Rajan: *Tell me, do you or do you not like talking to me?*

Mansa felt very scared, but at the same time did not want to offend or lose him. She was still very conscious about revealing her true feelings and thoughts to him.

She gave a non-committal 'Hmm'.

Rajan: *No hmm. Yes or no? Otherwise I am gone and then I won't care even if you come calling on me in your Ferragamos or Jimmy Choos.*

Mansa: *What are you talking about? You are so funny and*

that's why I enjoy talking to you. But I do have a pair of Jimmy Choos and I could come calling on you in those.

Rajan: *Oh, so you like talking to me. I feel lucky today. Just imagine if we had met in college.*

Mansa felt a bit confused, but added defiantly: *Well! We didn't.*

Rajan: *Oh! So, the privileged elite of Delhi even has a Jimmy Choo. By the way, what does your husband do?*

Mansa: *He works for an MNC as the COO.*

Rajan: *Oh there! I should have known. You live close to a golf course, husband COO in an MNC, daughter studying in UK. Why would you even care to talk to me?*

Mansa: *Hmm, again you are so full of LBS ego! You are the one who lives in LA and makes pots of money and that too in US dollars, and I have to hear all this. What does your wife do? Is she also an engineer?*

Rajan: *No, but she works.*

Mansa: *Oh, so you are loaded. Degree from LBS, earning NRI wife and you both live in LA.*

Rajan: *WHAT are you talking about?*

Mansa: *Exactly what you were saying.*

Rajan: *No harm in being a bit self-deprecating.*

Mansa: *Aren't you sleepy? It must be well after midnight. Want to say bye?*

Rajan: *No wait. I am not sleepy. I feel like getting wet with you in the rain.*

Mansa's heartbeat raced, as her cheeks felt aflame. She had never experienced such euphoria, and hated to admit to herself that she was enjoying it. She didn't know how to react.

Rajan: *You always ignore my question.*

Mansa: *What question?*

Rajan: *Should I repeat it? I keep talking to myself and you don't say anything.*

Mansa: *Say it. I have work to do, plus it's so late for you too.*

Rajan: *Say that you think of me. I really like you.*

Mansa kept quiet, feeling a bit uncomfortable.

Rajan: *Come on, say something, I want more.*

Mansa's heart was beating faster than it ever had. Feeling somewhat uneasy, she maintained her silence.

Mansa finally regained her composure and countered him: *Why are we talking like this? What are we doing? We have picture-perfect families.*

Saying this, she quickly logged out.

For the first time, a wave of guilt over her past week's behaviour engulfed her. Was she actually enjoying talking to a stranger more than she had enjoyed anything else in her life before? What was it that made her feel at one with him? Why did she feel pleasure in his company that she had never known before, even though she could not see him?

But her musings did not reduce her guilt. Nor could she extract a promise from herself that she would never talk to him again. For the first time in her life, she felt a lack of control. Increasingly, she found it difficult to concentrate on office or domestic work. She hated to admit her growing irresponsibility where Shonali was concerned. Not only had she reneged on her weekly outing plans with Shonali, opting for her long chats with Rajan instead (long, as she still typed very slowly). She also missed an important career-counselling parent–teacher meeting in school.

She cringed at the memory. Schools were about to reopen and a week before, the parents were called to school with their wards so that the child's subject stream could be decided with proper counselling in the parents' presence. Parents were asked to report at 10.30 a.m. Her mind, obsessed with Rajan, was looking for excuses to skip it.

Abruptly, at the door, she said, 'Abhi... oh I am so sorry. Shone, can you and Papa please manage together? I just got a call from Radhika; some important clients are coming to meet me in the office. You both will manage fine. I know it. Won't you?'

Abhijit's expression was one of absolute disbelief. 'Are you sure, Mansa?' he asked, 'Are your clients that important? It's a very crucial and life-defining moment in Shonali's life. Whether it was fever or any other crises, I don't ever remember you ever missing a single parent–teacher meeting for Malvika or Shonali.'

Mansa retorted angrily, 'Was I working then? What are you trying to say? If the clients were not so important, would I go just for fun?'

Shonali, who always got terrified at the possibility of any situation turning into a quarrel, quickly tried to soothe matters. 'Mom, it's really okay. Please don't worry.' And looking at Abhijit she said, 'Papa, we can manage just fine. As it is, I have decided to take commerce. How Maludi studies, terrifies me. So no science for me.'

Mansa couldn't stay beyond this as she wanted to reach her office as soon as possible lest the stranger disappeared to sleep. Such had become her morning chatting obsession with him that no matter whatever the urgency of things to do at that hour, she would ignore it in favour of chatting with him. A couple of times when she was late or caught in a jam, she would open her laptop in the car itself with a data card and start chatting.

Every night and morning when she logged in, she found her inbox loaded with sweet nothings from him. Half-indulgent, half-hesitant, attracted and entrapped in the magic weaver's web, she began with hesitant half-smiles and her hushed yeses soon became full smiles, and then grins and giggles. During the day, she would keep reminding herself of moral turpitude and forbid herself from indulging in what had become her daily ritual. But as soon as she entered office and the stranger came online, all resolve vanished.

This time again with great difficulty, she brought her mind back to her work. She was trying to decipher what Rajan meant by 'I want more'. Was her sixth sense correct in thinking that it had some perverted sexual meaning behind it? Or was she prejudging him? Slightly hesitant and a bit intrigued, she looked at her watch and saw that it was past noon. She hadn't looked at any work. Over the last few days, there had been several unanswered calls from friends waiting to be answered. Pratap, for instance, had called over six times, but she did not feel like talking to him.

Abhimansa, which she had started with great aspirations, seemed to have taken a back seat in her life and so had the entire real world, including her family and friends. She tried brushing Rajan off her mind—with limited success— and plodded through her work till evening. Many chores lay unattended even at home, as she spent more and more time chatting online with the stranger.

Once home, the only thing she eagerly awaited again was to catch up with Rajan even if for a few minutes before sleeping. As she clambered into bed, Abhijit appeared asleep. Comfortably at night when she logged in, she saw an unread message from their morning conversation: *We are playing with fire but I can't help thinking about you all the time.*

Soon the stranger himself was online.

Rajan: *Still awake?*

Mansa: *Why?*

Rajan: *You were used to sleeping early you had said.*

Mansa: *I was working, so decided to check my messages too.*

Rajan: *That's good. No harm in saying you were checking for me. Be a little kind to me also.*

Mansa remained silent.

Rajan: *Just a paratha and sari, and I am yours. It's just that I have a very modern wife.*

Nervously, Mansa tried to decipher what he meant. Afraid, Mansa typed: *I warned you in the morning to watch your words— we are married people.*

Mansa again felt a little confused and strange, but she knew his gibberish well by now and was kind of beginning to enjoy it. Whenever he wrote 'I am yours' her heart beat faster or completely stopped. She was enjoying that feeling. She found herself smiling many times whenever she thought of him.

Suddenly, she heard Abhijit breathe heavily. No sooner than she turned to look in his direction, he was shaking wildly and screaming in a loud voice, 'Noooooo noooo!' Instantly realizing that he was going through a frightening nightmare, she reached out to soothe him. Then he was up with a jerk, clasping Mansa in the fear caused by the dream, causing her laptop to fall down from her lap, shattering her intoxicated dreaminess.

She wrapped Abhijit in her arms for a few moments, not caring to look at the laptop, and soothed him back to sleep while gently stroking his forehead. She stretched close to him, helping him to drift back to sleep. Momentarily, she felt guilty and wondered if his recurrent bad dreams would ever come to an end. Although Abhijit's parents and Mansa had done their best by consulting the best psychiatrists and psychotherapists, nothing had worked to cure him of the nightmares.

But she could not push the thoughts of Rajan away from her mind. She felt that what she felt for him was what 'romantic love' would feel like. Although Abhijit and she had always agreed that romantic love did not exist, today Mansa could not hold on to her belief. She had been smitten and thought that it never did any harm for a husband to flirt a little with his wife, but injecting such sweeteners in the marriage was alien to Abhijit. In stark contrast, Rajan's affable style was only too suffused with romantic outpourings.

Mansa was suddenly reminded of a night, which still haunted her. She had been married to Abhijit for a couple of years and had thought she would try to spark some romantic interest in her husband. She wore a chic new black, lacy nightie with spaghetti straps, which showed off her svelte figure. Expecting to be praised and admired, she had lain down next to Abhijit and waited, but despite her best attention-seeking tactics, he had not even noticed her new nightie. In fact, did not react to her at all. He had just rolled over on his side, his back towards her and gone to sleep, snoring. She had wept most of the night, feeling miserable and humiliated.

There were many such painful memories, which hurt whenever they surfaced, even though she knew that Abhijit was a dutiful husband, a well-meaning person and a gentle soul, who never meant to hurt her or anyone intentionally but sometimes she was forced to wonder: did he have another love interest which he could never get over? Or had he never actually found her attractive?

And here was Rajan, she thought, ever ready with his insouciant romantic charm. How easy it was for Mansa to log off whenever she felt intimidated by the way he spoke and how difficult it was to shake him off her mind. It was beyond doubt that he had lit a fire in her. Even though she felt momentarily angered and logged out, the truth was that every time they chatted, he succeeded in fanning the fire.

Mansa felt as though the person she had waited subconsciously for all her life had arrived. And maybe this was the reason why she had not been able to like anyone else so far, because somewhere in the far recesses of her mind she had always known that he would find her someday. And now, she found it. But did she have it in her to give up everything for Rajan? Will she be able to leave everything to go away with Rajan if given a choice?

The answer was quite clear: No. She cannot leave her daughters, her husband, her family and her life.

And then, guiltily, she looked at Abhijit again, cursing herself and promising in her mind to never look in Rajan's direction again. Her eyes welled up and she rolled herself to look towards the floor below where the laptop had fallen. She had no idea if it had survived though it had fallen on the carpet beside her bed with the cover open. With her inner demons engulfing her senses, she had no energy and desire to pick the laptop. It certainly looked less bruised than her soul. She had no sleep that night.

The next day, as soon as she entered her office and proceeded towards her cabin, she was overwhelmed by her compulsion to check her messages. She, however, crushed her instincts as there were many pending mails to be answered, usual morning correspondence to be mailed to clients, new menus to be drafted and endless small and big chores. But not for very long; when it came to connecting with the stranger online everything else just didn't matter. As she logged in after a couple of hours, she saw that he had already been online for quite some time waiting for her. Her message box was swelling with couplets from him:

Dono jahan teri mohabbat mein haar ke
Woh jaa raha hai koi shab-e-gum guzaar ke

(Having forfeited both this world and the next for love's sake

There goes a sad soul with a sad night in his wake)

The couplet further saddened her.

When she did not react for some time, Rajan pinged her: *Mansa, where are you? I have been waiting.*

When she could no longer resist, Mansa typed: *You have*

promised to behave...

Rajan: *I was thinking if it was raining, we could get wet together.*

Even in her most depressive mood, the mischievous message caused a faint smile over her lips.

Mansa: *Well. There are no signs of rain here. There is still some time for the rainy season.*

Rajan: *I know that. Don't you have any imagination?*

He sounded annoyed to her.

Irritated with his tone, Mansa replied: *Yes, of course I do.*

Rajan: *Okay, forget it. I wish I could be on the dance floor with you. I like you. I want to look into your beautiful eyes. I am crazy about you. I think about you all the time.*

Instantly, Mansa lost her temper and she typed: *You are again talking like that. I hear that night time chatting is a favourite pastime of some men. You seem to have a PhD on women.*

Rajan: *What gives you the right to insult me like that? Why are you saying such hurtful things? I am trying to make you feel special and you are hurting me.*

Mansa: *I didn't mean to hurt you, but if we are to continue talking then don't say things that make me uncomfortable.*

Mansa logged out indignantly.

The next few days were hectic. She was unable to concentrate on work. His *sher-o-shayari* kept echoing in her ears. She was beginning to miss Rajan's presence in her real life. His impromptu poetry, wit, great sense of humour, romantic tone, and his flirting like a Casanova with his fans—everything about him attracted her, perhaps because he was the polar opposite of her husband. She feared Rajan, but at the same time felt a strong attraction towards him. She felt elated that he was the centre of attention for many females and she was becoming his centre of attention.

Yet again, she mused about Abhijit and her marriage, but the fact remained that they had never been romantically attracted to one another. She wondered how that gentle guy Pratap had courted her once, but she had felt nothing towards him. They had finally ended up being professional friends, so why were her inhibitions diluting now? Had she changed with the exposure to the world? Or was it because an online indulgence somehow seems safe and secret? She had no clue.

She was still in a flurry of thoughts when Radhika walked in with a document requiring her urgent intervention. She handed her an article draft, which was shortly due for submission as her column in a monthly lifestyle magazine, *Gourmet Delights*. Mansa worked till almost 6.30, but slipped into thoughts of Rajan every now and then. She had never been in such a state of mind before, sometimes enjoying it but also feeling annoyed at herself.

As she sat in the back seat of her car, she leaned her head back and closed her eyes. She was trying to conjure his image in her mind and mentally revisited their previous conversations. It was such a pleasant experience. Even though she had angrily logged out, he was lingering more on her mind than ever. When she reached home, she wondered if she should check that Rajan is online, but quickly dismissed the idea.

She went about every chore in a mechanical manner, submerged in his thoughts , knowing that in office she had not done any justice to the document Radhika had handed over to her. At 10 p.m., she sat on her bed with her legs stretched out and the laptop resting on her lap on a pillow to take care of the document. Guilt swept over her as she realized that she was lagging behind in every professional commitment. Her mind had stopped creating exotic recipes. These days it only triggered chemicals that caused romantic thoughts.

Abhijit hadn't joined her in the bedroom yet. She could hear him in the adjacent room chattering and laughing with Shonali over a platter of fruit. It was the beginning of the weekend. For years they had bid Shonali goodnight together over a platter of fruit during summer months (and hot milk in the winter). Today, Mansa heard the laughter as though it was coming from somewhere faraway. Why was she perched here with the laptop? Ideally, she should have been out there, sitting with her family and sharing the laugh. She should have been a part of the quiz ritual, where every night, Abhijit popped a few questions and Malvika, Shonali and Mansa would try to guess the answers, and if no one could crack them, then Abhijit pitched in the answers with great delight. The questions ranged from history and cinema to the latest inventions and discoveries on the science frontier. With time, the questions had been expanded to include nuances of macro and micro economics as well. Malvika and Shonali always looked forward to this family ritual.

Mansa and their daughters were very proud of Abhijit's enormous knowledge and his analytical skills regarding the Indian as well as world economy. After Malvika shifted to London, the audience for the questions had been reduced to Shonali and Mansa. A twinge of guilt touched Mansa's heart, but she did not budge from her position.

Even after almost an hour, she had very little success with the document, as her mind kept wandering to Rajan, who had not appeared online when she did check. The document was a guideline sketch for the next article on nutritive cooking, which Mansa contributed to *Gourmet Delights*. The next day was the deadline for the submission and she hadn't written a word. She waited for him and was feeling very angry and anxious. All sorts of thoughts crossed her mind, the most worrisome being, would she never hear from him again? The mere thought choked her senses.

Abhijit entered the room and sat beside her. 'What's keeping you so busy tonight?' he asked.

'Just my monthly column,' she said indifferently.

The clock on the wall showed that it 11.15. Yet there was no sign of the stranger online, leaving her feeling dull with disappointment. Ever since they had started chatting about a fortnight ago, this was the first time he had not come online. Despondently, she logged out and without answering Abhijit, lay down on the bed. Abhijit reached for her hand, but she gently pulled it away and closed her eyes, rolling away from him.

The dullness continued the next morning. She anxiously waited to find out what could have kept him away. It even crossed her mind that he might have lost interest in her, which made her feel more desolate than anything ever had.

She was so desperate to connect with him that she decided to give her morning jog a miss and stayed in bed on the pretext of work on her document, waiting for him to come online.

It was not to be. She fought to keep her tears from spilling out. She felt as though she had lost something very precious. After repeatedly being called by Abhijit and Shonali for breakfast, she dragged herself out of bed with great difficulty.

Bela was used to Mansa storming the kitchen over the weekends for close scrutiny and being scolded about matters ranging from the cleanliness of the kitchen to the menu for breakfast. An elaborate late lunch was usually planned, as dinner was mostly never at home on the weekends. Her absence from the kitchen surprised even Bela.

Shonali came to her and putting her arms around her neck, asked for the cheese rolls that Mansa usually made with Bela's help on the weekends. Today instead, she assigned Bela to make them without supervising her. She knew they would be a disaster without her help, but she couldn't care less. Even when they sat down for breakfast, Mansa had no interest in what had been arranged on the table. She barely ate a few morsels of her roll and excused herself, saying that she had too much work to take care of and retreated to her bed. This time she found him online. It must have been past midnight in LA, she thought.

Mansa quickly started the conversation: *Where have you been?*

Rajan: *I have been travelling. I have business presentations due.*

Mansa asked, agitatedly: *Why didn't you tell me?*

Rajan: *I travel almost three times a week. But I missed you all the while.*

Mansa: *Liar, then why didn't you talk to me yesterday?*

Rajan: *Again, see how you talk. I wanted to but was caught in too many things plus you say such hurtful things.*

Mansa: *I never meant to hurt you. I only wanted you to be*

careful about saying inappropriate things.

Rajan: *Oh THOSE things! ;) Then couldn't you say something softer, like a buddhu or something like that. Let's talk about something else…?*

Mansa: *Hmm, maybe. Where do you travel to?*

Rajan: *Midwest, Kansas and just about anywhere in the US.*

Mansa: *Where are you now?*

Rajan: *Just came back from a conference in Chicago.*

Mansa: *Hmm.*

Rajan: *Say something.*

Mansa: *What?*

Rajan: *Whatever you would like to say to me.*

Mansa: *I felt like talking to you.*

Rajan: **hug**

Mansa: *Again? A hi or hello is fine.*

Rajan: *Why can't I give you a hug?*

Mansa remained silent.

Rajan: *I know we both like each other. Chances are we would end up being close friends.*

Mansa: *Hmm, maybe!*

Rajan: *But I want more. I missed you. I am crazy about you.*

Mansa couldn't decide if she was angry or happy.

Mansa was trying to figure out what he meant, when he repeated: *I want more.*

She felt uneasy and thought that if she continued chatting with him, he might steer the conversation further in the same direction. She wondered if his words had any double meaning.

Rajan: *Why is it always me who has to do all the talking?*

Mansa: *It's not true. I am talking too.*

Rajan: *And suppose I say something which you won't like?*

Mansa: *Then don't say it.*

Rajan: *Look, I know I am just a person to pass time with for you. You have no feelings for me.*

Mansa: *Not true.*

Rajan: *Then why don't you show them? Why don't you say something nice to me? Why don't you make me feel special?*

Mansa: *You are a very special man, yes. But a man of honour will never cross the line to make me disrespect you or myself.*

There was a long silence.

Rajan: *Hmm, but you also said that I have many good points and you like the way I talk.*

Mansa: *Yes, except when you say certain things. This is not our age to get attracted to or get into a relationship with anyone.*

Rajan: *You have expectations.*

Mansa: *What? Expectations? What expectations? What can you give me that I don't have? Forget it. I am in a strange mood. I am working from home.*

Rajan: *Good. Good to work hard.*

Mansa: *It's not that.*

Rajan: *Then what?*

Mansa: *It's the document.*

Rajan: *What about the document now?*

Mansa: *I am not able to work on it. Just can't focus on anything. This has never happened before.*

Rajan: *Ha, good. Now work on it and complete it.*

Mansa: *Can't. I tried my level best. I even lost two kilos, which were not budging for a long time, without any effort. I have even lost my appetite. I feel so lethargic at times and don't feel like doing anything. Please stop talking the way you do, my focus goes missing. I have never felt like this before. I feel so guilty.*

Rajan: *Why do you feel guilty? And it's a good sign that you lost your appetite. Wait wait, there is someone here. I will be back. I am travelling for a conference again soon.*

Rajan logged out and a teary-eyed Mansa stayed online the entire day. Neither could she focus on the document nor did she hear from Rajan again.

In the evening, she found it strange that she had no desire for an outing and with great difficulty, Abhijit succeeded in convincing her to join him for a movie and dinner.

Abhijit said, 'Mana, let's go for a movie.'

Mansa replied, 'No Abhi... I would rather rest and work at home.'

He said gently, 'It's up to you... but Shona is very keen on a movie and this newly built Ambience Mall. What happened to your obsession with checking new stores? Shona needs an outing. She is particularly keen on watching *Life of Pi*. Are you getting ready? Should I book tickets?'

She dragged herself to the bathroom to dress quickly but could not get herself to be interested in the movie. Her mind kept wandering to Rajan and she only wanted to catch up with him online as early as possible. It was as if her life depended on it.

When late at night she logged in again, he was not online.

The next morning again began on a very low note for Mansa. She finished her gym routine exceptionally quiet and without much interaction with anyone. She was conscious of the trainer's questioning glances but chose to ignore them. She was in no mood to contribute to the Sunday breakfast at home either. She wandered in and out of her room with one eye on her laptop. She suddenly heard Shonali complain from the breakfast table, 'Oh my God! Vegetable rolls again today? Mom, couldn't you make something special today with cheese, please? It's Sunday!'

Mansa uncharacteristically charged in Bela's direction to know why she hadn't made something different. Bela sheepishly gave an easy excuse, 'There was so much left over from yesterday's breakfast. Plus I have chopped a variety of fruits and there is porridge too. ' Mansa walked out of the kitchen, feeling a little guilty but undeterred. Bela continued, 'You people hardly touched anything yesterday.' Mansa kept quiet, as she had no answer.

Mansa stayed at the dining table only toying with bits of food for a short while and then scurried to her room to go online to check if Rajan had logged in. She was not sure of finding him today, as she thought that he would be busy on a Saturday night. But she was in for a pleasant surprise. Both of them greeted each other excitedly.

Rajan: *Hey. Great to see you!*

Mansa: *Hi!*

Rajan: So what's up? Oh, just give me a minute, looks like my son just woke up.

Mansa: *Sure, run, or he might cry.*

Mansa could hear Abhijit calling out for her and felt that she should be sitting with her family, as it was a Sunday morning. But despite realizing this, she couldn't leave Rajan and go.

Rajan: *Mansaaa. What if we were close to each other, sitting together, our arms around each other?*

Mansa typed, her heart melting like butter, hormones surging: *Well good we aren't and I told you not to talk to me like this.*

Rajan: *You don't even want to talk to me. Whenever I try to say something you just log out.*

Mansa: *Why do you say things that make me uncomfortable? Talk about something else.*

Rajan: *Like what?*

Mansa: *Like anything. Okay, what did you eat for dinner?*

Rajan: *Grilled fish. And you?*

Mansa: *Vegetable cheese rolls, not your paratha. I am a vegetarian.*

Rajan: *Bye, I am sleepy.*

Mansa: *Why so early? We did not even talk yesterday.*

Rajan: *You don't like the way I talk.*

Mansa: *That's not true.*

Rajan: *Then why do you always log off and not make me feel special? Look, I have plenty of friends. I don't want a weather-talking friend. I see you as special, someone very special and want to be seen like one too.*

Mansa: *Of course, you are also a special friend.*

Rajan: **tight hug**

Mansa: *Stop trying to come close to me. I just told you it makes me uncomfortable.*

Rajan: *You also agreed you are a special friend. Then you have to let me say what I like.*

Mansa: *Bye, I am going out with my family.*

Her heart beating wildly, Mansa logged out.

Only two thoughts prevailed in her mind these days. One was Rajan, and the other was why she felt like an obsessive romantic at her age, especially when she had never felt any such emotion before. She tried shaking him off her mind, but could not succeed.

The next day in office, catching up with him was again the first thing she wanted to do. Once online, she found a popular Bollywood song awaited her:

> *Chhoti-chhoti baatein yunhi aate-jaate Yaadein*
> *sehlaake jaati hai*
> *Raaton ko sirhaane baasi muskaane Mujhko sula ke*
> *jaati hai*
> *Milna nahin hai mumkin itna bataaun lekinHum phir*
> *mile kyun hain*
> *Tujhko bula naa paaun tujhko bhula naa paaun*
> *Yeh silsile kyun hain Sab kuch wahi hai, par kuchh*
> *kami hai*
> *Teri aahatein nahin hai Sab kuch wahi hai, par kuchh*
> *kami hai*
> *Teri Aahatein nahin hai.. nahin hai*

(Every big and small thing I encounter in my life these days reminds me of you and however much I may try to sleep, sleep eludes me without you. It's impossible to meet; then why have we met...)

And soon, Rajan Chopra emerged online and Mansa again found herself mesmerized by the song and its sender. She stared hard at the picture of his son, trying to imagine what he might look like. She was engrossed in reading the poetry, her eyes becoming damp. Then he suddenly wrote something that shook her.

Rajan: *I am thinking all the wrong things about you.*

Mansa froze. Feeling violated, as though her worst fear had come true, she vented out: *You are free to think whatever you like in your mental space. Why are you telling me this?*

Rajan was like a whirlpool, which was drowning Mansa. Unable to think straight, she deleted him at once and logged out, promising herself that she would never speak to him again, no matter what. She was overcome with a restlessness she had never experienced and in a state of agitation, her tears crazily fell. Ever since she had started chatting, deep down she had feared that he might turn out to be someone who preyed on women. She had read in newspapers and heard from friends about the presence of such predators online and also about the steadily increasing cyber-crime rate against women and children across the world. She knew that if he ever hurt her married sensibilities, she would be left with little choice but to delete him, and that was something she did not want in the least.

Yet she had been so captivated by his amorous conversation and talking to him seemed like the best time she had ever had. After deleting him, she felt miserable and utterly disconsolate. Tears from her eyes did not stop rolling down the entire day. The enormity of her feelings for him terrified her. She had many questions for herself, but no answers.

Glumly, she got through the day as it graduated towards evening.

Her restlessness kept growing with each moment. She faced

the growing challenge of having to put him out of her mind. She was strongly aware of her failure in achieving this.

At night when she opened her laptop, a message was waiting for her. She had decided to never read his messages again. She tried to resist the temptation to find out what he might have written and logged out quickly—but not for long. At around 10 p.m., she logged in again with unusual trepidation, after promising herself that she would not respond to him even if she read what he had written. There, awaiting her, was a long message, almost like a letter.

Mansa,

I have been trying to be friends with you as I thought we both liked each other.

Your thinking is wrong. I told you I see you as someone very special and care about you and told you to not judge me, but even then you criticized me.

It's wrong to believe that I have some evil designs on my mind. However, I don't see why I have to bear these repeated insults. I haven't given you or anyone else the right to insult me or to assassinate my character.

I even warned you before that I can't bear this hurtful behaviour any more, but you continue to hurt me.

You will always stay with me like a good memory. I can't go through this turmoil again. So let's move on.

I wish you well in life.

Yours,
Rajan Chopra

Mansa broke down as soon as she read it. She felt as though his feelings for her were as intense and true as hers for him and she was insulting his intentions by continuously being suspicious of him. She tossed and turned in her bed at night with a heavy burden on her heart. She hated herself for deleting him in haste. She kept praying to God that something magical should happen to make Rajan add her back. But she did not receive any more messages from him.

Mansa could not work the next day. Her eyes felt continually damp. She started to reason out in her brain how she could restore communication with him in a dignified way and decided on replying to him with a warning that he would never trespass the line of respect and trust as they were both responsible and married people.

However, when she finally addressed him, to her disbelief, she wrote in a way she hadn't intended to: *Stop talking to me and go and make as many online conquests as you want. It is not as if we are at the point of no return.*

She had expected some relief from her heart after her outpouring, but there was none. Instead, it seemed to infuriate him further. Within minutes, she had a nasty reply from him:

You can make as many conquests as you like. I did not say anything inappropriate. I was just being friendly but that is something beyond your understanding.

Mansa felt petrified. She found it hard to believe that someone who's been chatting with her animatedly for weeks saying things as intimate as paratha and sari; getting wet in the rain; I am yours, I want more ; and mailing poetry so casual?

This kind of retaliatory tone was something new to her,

as she had spent her life with someone very gentle. She felt angry enough to block him this time, but wrote back before that: *So what were all those sweet nothings from you? What are we trying to do? Indulging in mudslinging! While I accepted my mistake, you behave as though you did nothing wrong. Please grow up Mr Rajan Chopra—it takes two to tango.*

She found no peace after she messaged him. She kept crying secretly, fearing deep down that she may never hear from him again. The retributive language of his reply caused her tears to roll down for days to come. On top of that, she was dealing with the agony of not being able to connect with him and fearing she had lost him forever. Her heart desperately prayed for him to be back.

She wanted to believe that maybe something was wrong with her, and maybe she was too rigid and his was a socially acceptable way of flirting and socializing. It was she who was outdated, out of the loop for too long, a relic, a fossil.

She also wondered why this recent relationship was causing her so much anguish, unable to realize that when the social networking site had become her parallel universe and thought sphere, emotions attached to the virtual world had taken over the concrete reality in which she lived.

Finally, after many days, she heard from him.

Rajan: *Talking to you, I feel as though I am talking to a twelfth standard child. You just don't understand my feelings for you.*

A desperate Mansa, dying to have him back in her life, answered: *It was an attention-seeking tantrum as you had been quiet for two days and I couldn't bear it. But, I never expected such a sharp reaction from you. Why were we in a blame game?*

I respect you. It was a mistake to misjudge/ judge you. I know you are a thorough gentleman and would never do anything to make me disrespect you or myself. With this belief I am adding you back.

To make him feel most special, she typed: *You are the first male I have added.*

Showing his stubbornness, although he kept messaging her, he did not add her back. When two days passed since she had sent the request, angry and hurt, Mansa withdrew her friend request.

Another day passed by. Finally in the evening, she was pleasantly surprised to see his request waiting for her and immediately added him back. Rajan had also added an apology for his harsh and rude language.

Rajan: *What you thought about me was absolutely wrong. I really respect you. I will never hurt you. It's strictly between us, you and me. I can never ever imagine harming you. Give me your email id.*

Mansa: *Why?*

Rajan: *I don't want to lose you ever. Can't go through it again.*

Mansa: *Take both my ids. Do you want my cell number too?*

Rajan: *No, I don't want to complicate things for you.*

He sounded so sincere and noble to Mansa that she began blindly trusting in him even more, the residual traces of doubts and misgivings about him dispelled from her mind. Their bond was now much stronger than before and Mansa's happiness was returning.

Abhijit and Shonali were happy to see Mansa glowing. Mansa felt a tad guilty when Abhijit told her how wrong he had been in keeping her home all these years. 'It's the pleasure of working that gives you so much of happiness,' he said.

As Mansa realized her growing attraction towards the stranger online, she started oscillating between moments of deep guilt and pure bliss. She was not sure how she was supposed to handle this experience.

Mansa was a typical sapiosexual. Nothing dim or mundane held her attention for long. But now, she seemed quite different. She had tried resisting Rajan in her natural manner by keeping quiet, but she could not bring herself to ignore him. She soon found herself answering his long poetic discourses and did not even realize when her feelings towards him changed. Rajan had been admirable in his persistence.

Torn between right and wrong, she often decided to not respond to Rajan, but her resolution never lasted for long.

8

The Parallel World

'I love you without knowing how, or when, or from where.
I love you simply, without problems or pride: I love you in
this way because I do not know any other way of loving
but this, in which there is no I or you, so intimate that
your hand upon my chest is my hand, so intimate that
when I fall asleep your eyes close.'

—Pablo Neruda

WAS RAJAN CHOPRA honest in his revelations to her or was he
a cad who only loved himself and talked romantically with every
available female? Mansa was imagining the worst; even though
they had been chatting for over six weeks, was it possible he
was simply flirting, out to have a good time online, while she
was genuinely getting attached to him? Nonetheless, with his
presence in her life she always felt on cloud nine.

As office and home were both taking a back seat in

comparison to Rajan, she even feared how she would survive if she lost him. Where was their relationship going?

She reached her office, anxious thoughts clouding her mind, *Does he genuinely care about me? How will I ever know? Why am I not able to stop myself from getting more involved?* Disturbed to her very soul, she opened her chat window to find Rajan already online.

Rajan: *I just dreamt about you.*

Mansa smiled, feeling an exhilarating shiver. She typed: *Dream? About me? What dream?*

Rajan: *I saw that we were together on a dance floor. Dancing closely and looking very lovingly into each other's eyes and you suddenly bent my head in your direction to kiss me.*

Mansa agitatedly typed: *Keep quiet! Keep quiet! Stop your overtures or I will go completely incommunicado. Why would I do that? I have told you umpteen times not to talk to me like this.*

Rajan: *Fine, fine. I know. I will not talk about it. But please don't log out again.*

One day, she actually found him online very late in the morning. She instantly messaged: *What are you doing online at this time?*

Rajan: *You tell me what I am doing this late...waiting for you, of course.*

Rajan: *Do you like me?*

Mansa: *I do, but...it's not appropriate. And we are not getting any younger. It's really late for you. Please don't be up on my account.*

Rajan: *Do you care?*

Mansa: *Yes, of course. I can't have you up this late waiting for me, makes me feel guilty.*

Rajan: *The day seems like a punishment when I don't connect with you.*

Mansa: *To me too*

Rajan: *Am I allowed to put my arms around you? Promise me that you will never do this again.*

Mesmerized, Mansa typed: *Do what?*

Rajan: *You very well know what I mean. Stop talking to me all of a sudden.*

Mansa: *Does it matter?*

Rajan: *Of course it does. I care about you...promise me. Promise me and are you still in my arms?*

Mansa: *Then you also promise to not cross your limits.*

Rajan: *Promise, only if you will believe me.*

The cycle of chatting resumed—and with it returned Mansa's lost happiness.

The next morning as she entered her office, her assistant Radhika handed her an envelope. A big international culinary event was going to be organized in Delhi and Gary Om was on the managing committee of the event. The prestigious partnership invite to co-host the event had been extended to Abhimansa. Her entire team was looking up to her for a green signal to participate and the prospect looked extremely tempting, ambitious though it was. Willy-nilly the Abhimansa team got into it. An excited exchange of ideas about the upcoming event was on in her room. But her mind was in a territory only she knew of—the formidably charming Rajan Chopra. She desperately waited for them to wind up and leave her alone.

Finally, when she had the opportunity to log in, he was not online. She left him a message.

Mansa: *Where are you?*

She got back a response only at night.

Rajan: *I am attending an important technology annual event, Techno Sapphire.*

Mansa: *Techno Sapphire? What is that?*

There was no response and suddenly Rajan went offline.

Annoyed, Mansa typed: *Bye.*

After a long time he resurfaced. *Rajan: Ohh…an annual event where technology companies showcase the best possible ways of storing big data. And I have people around. I am not ignoring you. I am missing you. I wish I could be with you at a candlelight dinner;). Will be back soon. Bye for now.*

Charmed again, she stayed online, revisiting their conversations and checking out the profiles of his friends for most of the day. At night, she didn't realize when she had dozed off, waiting for him to come online.

The next morning, Abhijit asked, 'How come your laptop was lying open between us the entire night?'

Mansa retorted, 'I had a deadline for an article and was trying to finish it. Then I probably just dozed off.'

Out of genuine concern, Abhijit said, 'It's all right to work, but working that late will not only strain your eyes, it will also ruin your health and beauty, Mana.'

Mansa snapped angrily, 'You never want me to work!'

Later on, she had felt quite ashamed at her outburst. When she reached office and logged in she felt very lucky. Rajan was online, waiting for her.

Mansa: *Hi! How's the conference going?*

Rajan: *I am in the hotel. Was just thinking about you. I am missing you.*

Come to me. I am drunk. I want to make love to you.

Mansa: *What are you saying? Please just go away!*

Before she could realize, she logged off from the chat. The words echoed in her head, and she grew restless. Unable to sleep a wink, she looked like death warmed over.

Radhika asked her, 'Ma'am, if you are unwell, we could discuss it tomorrow.'

She was trying to be as normal as possible, but it wasn't working. So she feebly replied, 'It's just a mild headache, but yes, please let's do this tomorrow.'

That day, she thought about the whole situation till she almost passed out. Realizing that Rajan will never pay heed to her umpteen requests, she resolved to stop talking, at whatever cost. This time she was determined to keep her resolve.

Summer went by, making way for the pleasant monsoon months in Delhi. Mansa's veranda overlooked the lush garden track of the golf course and the cool scented breeze from the garden filled her home. The view of the golf course from her windows looked breathtaking, but the nature lover in Mansa felt hollow.

The preparations for the conclave were in full swing in Mansa's office. But her abilities and faculties were at an all-time low. Ever since she had fallen into the chatting cycle with Rajan she had completely cut herself from the real world. Work-related and even personal calls, all mostly remained unanswered and she had got more and more sucked into the cyber world.

Of all her friends, Sapna had noticed her becoming less and less communicative and unavailable on the phone or even for an occasional outing. She had been constantly calling to know if Mansa was well or had any pressing worry in her life so Mansa decided to visit Sapna one evening. She needed to talk about the Rajan issue and to find some way of dealing with the magnitude of her emotions.

She knew that for the past few months, Sapna had moved along with her children into a nice spacious house of her own in Sushant Lok. She had invited Mansa many times to come over but for Mansa, the time for real relationships had shrunk. But today she had such a heavy heart that she really needed a shoulder to cry on. The whole day she mulled over whether she should or should not confide in her friend.

She called Sapna to tell her that she would visit her straight from the office. Excited and eager to have her over, Sapna promised to reach home around the same time as her. When Mansa reached there and rang the doorbell, a matronly woman in her early seventies answered the bell. She resembled Sapna so much that Mansa knew that she had to be Sapna's mother. The old lady welcomed her warmly, hugged her and said, 'You must be Mansa. I have heard a lot about you from Sapna.'

Sapna's daughter was away to a boarding but her son was home. Jay, Sapna's son, was almost fourteen but perched on a wheelchair didn't look beyond nine. He smiled at her as she reached out to hug him and hand over a packet of chocolate.

Soon the doorbell rang again and Sapna entered, excitedly greeting Mansa. She hugged her son and mother before ushering Mansa to her bedroom for an intimate conversation.

They had a lot to talk about from Pratap, Gary Om, Tushita and many common friends to the personal story of Sapna. Sapna confided that unable to cope with her husband's jealousy over her flourishing career and his unreasonable demands on her time and money with nil participation in bringing up the children, she had taken the bold step of moving out and requested her mother to live with her for her son's sake.

Mansa did understand the challenges Sapna might be going through but her own grief about the relationship with Rajan made her less receptive to the problems in other people's lives. Meanwhile, the maid brought tea and some snacks made by Sapna's mother.

Sapna said with concern, 'Mansa, are you okay? You behave and look so different. How have you lost so much weight? Your slight chubbiness suited you perfectly well. Are you over-exercising or there is something else going on?'

Mansa was not sure where to begin or whether to share her devastation at all. Finally, she blurted out, 'I am in a relationship.'

Sapna was startled, 'What? Unbelievable! You have Abhijit as a husband, one of the finest men I know. Since when, and how? I should have guessed. Is it Pratap?'

Mansa shook her head. 'No.'

Sapna asked, 'Then who? How did you both meet?'

Mansa sheepishly replied, 'We met online.'

Sapna was horrified, 'Oh no. A woman of your stature and character befriended someone online? I don't believe this. And you are calling it a relationship? You know the implication and meaning of what you are saying? Don't you know how very dangerous it could be? I am not saying it's uncommon but it is certainly not meant for someone like you who's had domestic happiness for so many years with a doting husband like Abhijit.'

Mansa said, 'I tried controlling it many many times but failed. I feel such a strong soul connect that all my logic fails. Please help—what should I do? If I don't hear from him regularly I feel like dying. I lose all interest in life.'

Sapna cautioned, 'If you can take it casually and in a spirit of fun and as an experiment then fine, otherwise get out of it as soon as you can. Don't you know how men prowl for unsuspecting women online and can be very dangerous?'

Mansa said, 'He is a family man. Seems like a very fine person.'

Sapna frowned, 'Mansa, you have hardly seen the world. I know this type only too well. I myself chatted a bit with men a decade back when all this technology was new. You have been exposed to internet only now. And hardly understand the ways of either the real or virtual world.'

Mansa knew Sapna was talking sense and made a resolve to pay heed to her friend's advice. Time just flew as they chatted about other matters. Catching-up with each other's lives. Shonali and Abhijit called on her cell a couple of times so refusing Sapna's offers of dinner she moved towards her car. On her way home, she felt grimmer and unsure.

For almost two weeks, she had avoided and ignored all communication from Rajan, although she couldn't resist the temptation of visiting his profile and his group a few times a day. Once, as she and Rajan both logged on to the group almost concurrently, he posted:

> *gulo me rang bhare baad-e-nau-bahaar chale chale bhi*
> *aa o ke gulashan kaa kaar-o-baar chale*
> *qafas udaas hai yaaro sabaa se kuchh to kaho kahi to*
> *bahar-e-khudaa aaj zikr-e-yaar chale*
> *jo ham pe guzari so guzari magar shab-e-hijraan hamaare*
> *ashk teri aakabat sanwar chale*
> *makaam 'faiz' ko_i raah me janchaa hi nahi jo ku-e-yaar*
> *se nikale to su-e-daar chale*

> (Let the blooms fill with colour, let the first zephyr of spring flow
> Do come over, so the garden can get on with its daily business
> Gloom reigns in the cage, my love; so say something to the breeze
> Somewhere, for God's sake, there must be a talk about my beloved today
> I may have endured whatever i endured, but on the night of separation,
> My tears left your future course adorned
> No site no destination enroute caught the fancy, Faiz
> After quitting the beloved's lane, I walked to the gallows)

She had cried instead of replying. Copiously and piteously, as if her world was ending.

Time seemed to be drifting for Mansa in her depressed

state. Abhijit and Shonali were once again confused about Mansa's on again/off again mood, but did not pry much. More days passed by and she continued ignoring Rajan's inbox messages, which had by then become infrequent.

Almost a month had gone by since they had last chatted. The immense grief she was feeling was similar to what she had felt when her parents were killed in a sudden accident. She was quite sure by now that her relationship with Rajan had definitely ended. After a long time, she visited his profile—and his status message tore up her heart.

Ragon mein dorte phirne ke ham nahi qayal
Jab aankh se hi na tapka tu phir laho kya hai

(We are not convinced of its running and coursing in the veins
if it can't not drip from the eye, then is it blood?)

It was a Persian couplet. As she didn't understand the language fully, she mistakenly interpreted it to mean that he was shedding tears of blood for her. Another posted Urdu couplet she interpreted as,

I stand accused of a crime of passion.
And I will have to pay the price by giving my life.
And there are people who will never understand and be
unaffected whether I live or die.

On reading this, her torment knew no end. She had never felt so moved and helpless before. She could not stop crying and blamed herself endlessly for being rigid, over-suspicious and the cause for his depressive state of mind. He loved and cared for her as much as she did for him and she could not even fulfil his wish that she would talk to him. What if he did something to harm himself? How would she ever forgive herself?

Her fingers flew on the keyboard: *How are you? Hope you are fine.*

Rajan: *What do you care? Who am I to you? I am a joke to you. A means to pass your idle hours. What do you care if I live or die? You can start or stop talking to me any time, I am nothing to you.*

The lines tore her heart apart and she hastily typed: *Please don't say such things. It's difficult for me to conceive of any relationship online. We are married and very responsible people and there are several lives attached to us.*

Rajan: *Being married doesn't mean that we are dead. Married people can have feelings too.*

Mansa was taken aback at the statement but at same time could not negate its logic. She did not know what to say. It was in sharp contrast to how she had been raised and recklessly falling in love was not exactly how morality worked in her part of the world. She had been raised to believe that marriage was the most sacred institution, a bond for life. She did not understand what she was doing with this stranger. Why was she not able to stop herself? She belonged to Abhijit. He was such a fine human being and a good husband. How could she talk so animatedly with a stranger? The same guilt again engulfed her.

Mansa: *I have never gone through these emotions before. I have never gone out with anyone. I have never talked to anyone so much before. I have never even thought of another man before. It's all so complicated. All I know is that I really enjoy talking to you and spending time with you and when I can't reach you, my soul pierces me from within.*

Rajan: *Mine too. What has happened has happened. I have given myself up to fate.*

Mansa: *Fait accompli.*

She wondered what made her say that. She had never intended saying it, but she had and now there was no denying it or turning back. First, she had uploaded a photograph of hers in a sari when he praised her, and now she'd said these words. She did not understand what unseen force was making her do these things. It felt like some kind of commitment, a vow, like the merging of two souls.

When she woke up the next morning, the effect of the conversation still lingered on her mind. As soon as she reached office, she logged into her chat first thing.

Mansa: *Hi.*

Rajan: *Hi, Kanha is still playing. Not ready for sleep yet.*

Mansa: *Let him be. Don't push him too much to sleep. I am right here, not going anywhere.*

She felt a surreal affection for Kanha whenever she chatted with Rajan. She felt that Kanha was her own, and loved him like that.

Rajan had sensed her reservations and respecting this, seemed to have become less impassioned in voicing his expectations of her. He messaged her morning and evening, but a fragile balance of not crossing a certain mark had been created. Mansa had never liked her life better. She began to dread Saturdays and Sundays, as she feared that they would take away the comfort of chatting from office. Their bond was growing thicker by the day. However, she was miles away from focusing on her upcoming conclave and even on her culinary column for *Gourmet Delights*.

It had now been several months since Rajan and Mansa had met online. Mansa wondered how, even though the outside world was the same, her inner world had changed drastically in the past few months. She only hoped that no one at home had any clue about it.

One morning, after some urgent bank work, she reached her office much later than her usual 10 a.m. and hurriedly went to her cabin. She felt a little invaded as she was greeted by her team sitting inside, waiting to take her advice on some critical issues related to the forthcoming conclave. In a hurry to open her message box, she sounded lame even to her own ears, when she said, 'Give me ten minutes with my daughter; it's an emergency. I will join you soon, team!'

Radhika, the senior-most in her team, looked at her disbelievingly. A person, for whom work had been the first priority till some time back, wanted to postpone discussing a matter of such importance. With the question very apparent in her eyes, she left Mansa's cabin quietly.

As their footsteps faded, Mansa wondered if her team knew that she was chatting daily for a couple of hours at least. But there she was, consumed in chatting obsessively with the stranger again only seconds later. She was losing most of her crucial morning working hours, as he was losing his sleeping hours.

As she logged in, a sweet message awaited her.

Rajan: *Mansa, wonderful to 'see' you.*

Mansa: *Rajan, good to see you too.*

Rajan: *Imagine we were neighbours and you visit me when it is raining.*

Mansa felt completely spellbound. Blushing, she felt like a teenager—what she had missed in her younger years was happening now. Her body felt hot and she couldn't deny that despite her million denials and conscience pricks, she was physically attracted to the stranger. He captured her every free moment, infusing warmth in her.

However, terrified that he may take his physical suggestions further, she instantly logged out. Whenever he expressed a desire for intimacy verbally, she felt extremely terrified. It always led to a quarrel and a terse reaction from him.

His standard reactions were: *Let's move on, we are done, I will never talk to you.*

After which they would make up. All of this was by now routine and commonplace, but they always made it a point to resolve the issue quickly and even apologized to resume from where they had left off. Unknowingly, the relationship was getting stronger and the stranger was inching forward deeper into her life. In almost six months, a very strong bond had formed between them.

The next morning Mansa once again logged in to start chatting.

Mansa: *Hi.*

Getting no reply from Rajan, Mansa typed again: *Don't*

want to say hi to me?

Rajan: *You don't like my ways of saying hi. And I am tired of your unceremonious log offs. It feels like a one-way street. Bye. Good night.*

MansaHmm, my day has just started and we haven't talked. And you're already saying goodbye.

Rajan: *I can't do one way talking any more. I am tired of being just a filler in your day and hearing that you feel guilty.*

Mansa: *Please don't say that. Okay, I will talk. Tell me which movie did you see last?*

Rajan: I Hate Love Stories. *Was a good movie and suits you well.*

Mansa: *Very true. Love is only for celluloid, prose and poetry. I don't believe in it.*

Rajan: *Goodnight then. I am sleepy.*

He logged out suddenly. Dismayed, Mansa tried to distract herself by concentrating hard on the rising pile of work before her. Strangely, the very work that some time back had given a new direction and momentum to her life had become relegated to the back seat. Now, Rajan seemed to be her lifeline and the most important part of her life. She was beginning to realize that she was as much hopelessly in love with him as he was with her. She waited the entire day, but he did not appear online again that day.

The next morning, as expected, the day had a dreary start. She stepped into her office cabin without even caring to glance at the accumulating pile of documents needing her attention. The only urge she had was to log in to see if Rajan was online and had left her a message. He wasn't there and there was no message either. Unable to connect with him, she spent the wearisome day anxiously waiting for the evening.

Finally, unable to resist, she messaged him: *Why so much silence? Please say something.*

Rajan: *I don't know what to say. You find everything offensive. You don't like the way I talk. Let's move on.*

Mansa: *Why are you saying such hurtful things?*

Rajan: *Why don't you understand that I can't talk unnaturally? It's natural for me to want to come close to you. I care deeply about you and I am a very physical person. I crave for you.*

Mansa, feeling deeply anguished and hurt, typed: *Even I hate not being in touch with you. It feels so lonely and incomplete. But what you said just now makes me want to run away from you.*

Rajan: *I can't stay a single day without talking to you and thinking of you but you just ruin everything. Come on make me feel special.*

Mansa: *Let's promise that we will never fight again.*

Rajan: *You promise, you are the one who fights. I can't believe this. You are the most immature forty-five-year-old I know.*

Mansa: *My daughters also say, grow up, Mom, grow up. But you are in a quarrelsome mood and I have work waiting.*

Rajan: *I am sleepy too. I am going to sleep and dream of you.*

They both logged out at the same time, Mansa scared where he might take the conversation further. Mansa, by now, had completely formed a habit wanting Rajan to be present all the time. He had become her fixed and most inescapable routine. Her days were spent blushing over the messages she saw morning and evening. On one mental plane, she abhorred her weakness, but subconsciously she waited for the time she could be with her most special person. Caught between the morality of marriage and what she believed to be her true love, she was going through a personal hell of emotional crises. Finally, convincing herself that love was the most pious and fundamental of all emotions, she slowly started feeling less guilty.

At times, she often asked herself how a woman of her age and conservative, traditional Hindu upbringing could lose control over herself in this manner. Only God knew how this mysterious connection with an invisible and unseen man gave her such happiness. His orchestration of romance was so perfect that it swept Mansa completely off her feet, transporting her into a world of sensuality, romance and tenderness, which she had only seen in films. Rajan had touched her life in more ways than one, drenching her in this newfound love.

They had never met and Mansa did not even know what he looked like, yet he had woven magic in such a manner that he was always around her in all her conscious and unconscious moments. His jugglery with words was perfect. Sometimes he bent to kiss her on a dance floor, and at other times she was at a candlelit dinner with him. If she was angry with him, he had his arms around her.

Monsoon magic had kept them glued to poetic conversations about clouds, greenery, ghazals and poetry. She herself was thrilled at this quixotic discovery in herself, how much she enjoyed the romance. His words held an element of innocence and a strange mix of naughtiness.

Domestic duties, home, family, friends, socializing, entertainment, and the newly found joy of work had all diminished in comparison to the pleasure she derived from connecting with him. On one such morning, she found a long message from Rajan: *It's raining here and it is lovely. I can't think of anything besides you. I think of you all the time. I crave for you. I can never have enough of you. It's like being in college again. I didn't know I had so much desire in me. How I wish I could be with you. Listen to this song I am sending you. I have been listening to it and thinking of you. Imagine us together, just as the lovers in the song are. Hear it now.*

Mansa nervously typed: *Oh… I am in my office. I can't right now.*

Rajan: *Oh please, don't you have earphones?*

Mansa tried opening the link with trembling hands.

Her curiosity skyrocketing, Mansa said: *It's a link—is it a Rajesh Khanna song?*

Rajan was amused: *Oh, I didn't know that he was a singer.*

Mansa: *Oh, I think I did something wrong. Oh God, if someone comes here they will think all I do is chat and listen to filmy songs in my cabin. Oh, I am so dumb with technology.*

She listened to the song:

Ke tera zikr hai
Ya itr hai
Jab jab karta hoon
Mehekta hoon, Behekta hoon, Chehekta hoon Sholon ki tarah
Khusbuon mein dehekta hu
Behekta hu, Mehekta

Mansa: *Great lyrics, lovely dance. How come I haven't heard it before?*

Rajan: *Oh! So you are listening. They are my true feelings for you. It encapsulates all my feelings for you.*

Mansa: *I don't quite understand all of it. Too much Urdu for me.*

Rajan:
'Is it your mention, or some perfume whenever I do (mention)
I smell good, I get intoxicated, I chirp.
Like fireballs,
I get inflamed in scents,
I get intoxicated, I smell good..
Is it the worry about you, or pride,
whenever I do (worry) I go wayward, I jump, I slip,
Like mad, enjoying, I walk, I jump, I slip...

Mansa felt happiness flood her. From now on she decided to always keep earphones in her bag. But yet again unable to express her joy, feeling extremely awkward about the suggestive implications, she had logged out.

It had been a week and she had waited and waited morning and evening but there had been no sign of the stranger online. Her sadness deepened. This time, he had not bothered to woo her back. It was a Monday morning in office when at last she saw him online.

Mansa: *Hi.*

Rajan didn't reply.

Mansa waited for a while and when there was no response, messaged again: *Rajan, why don't you understand?*

Rajan: *Why don't you understand? We are done. Move on. I told you before if you log off without replying then that's it. It's over. I don't see why I should put up with such behaviour.*

Mansa: *Okay please, we could still be good friends.*

Rajan: *No, I don't need a friend.*

Mansa: *Don't be so heartless. Okay, you are my special friend.*

Rajan: *Friend? I don't need one. I told you.*

Mansa: *Okay, you are someone special.*

Rajan: *I AM TIRED OF HEARING THAT YOU ARE GUILTY AND OF YOUR LOG-OFFS. YOU HAVE TO UNDERSTAND. HERE WE HAVE ONLY THE WRITTEN WORD AS WE CAN'T SEE AND READ EACH OTHER'S EXPRESSION OR BODY LANGUAGE. YOU WILL HAVE TO BE MORE CANDID IN EXPRESSING YOUR FEELINGS.*

Mansa started sobbing: *I am trying. I am really trying. It takes time to change. I have never had a boyfriend or gone out even once with anyone except my sisters or husband but I am trying to change.*

Rajan: *Then why do you log off when I try to express myself?*

Mansa: *I feel very scared and improper.*

Rajan: *Mansa, please understand. I repeat: I will never hurt you or harm you. I really care about you. I respect our families. It's between us. It will never go anywhere.*

Mansa felt more anguished than ever. She thought that this was the root cause; he did not understand that it was not her husband or family that caused her to pull back, but the fact that it had to be a secret relationship, as though it was dirty or sinful. He did not understand that it was the moral breach in a marriage that terrified her. She had not once thought about the consequences of exposure, of her family finding out about it.

If it was love, the most sacred emotion, then why was it accompanied by fear? But she couldn't say it in so many words. It all stayed locked in her heart. Whatever his feelings for her were—true or untrue—she knew that she had found her soul-stirring true love in him.

Rajan: *As usual, you are quiet now. At least say something.*

Mansa: *I was thinking.*

Rajan: *What?*

Mansa: *So many lives depend upon us. What are we doing talking to each other for hours? Where are we going? We must stop.*

Rajan: *That's why I say you are scared to express yourself. We can't spoil our present for an unseen future.*

Mansa: *Raj, I was thinking, whenever one of us is angry the other quickly gives justifications and tries to make amends. We have no moral or legal binding to do that. Yet we always make up.*

Rajan: *THAT is why, that's why I say we both intensely care about each other. It's only you who holds back from expressing your feelings.*

Mansa: *I need time. I am improving. Now I try to be less shy and more expressive. I even express my likes on FB love songs.*

Rajan: *Then promise that you will never log off abruptly.*

Mansa: *You too promise you will not be angry. Whatever happens, permanent detachment is not possible?*

Rajan: *Yes, promise. Permanent detachment is not possible.*

Mansa: *I am emotionally very weak. Promise me that you will never hurt me.*

Rajan: *Promise, I will NEVER hurt you. Good night. It's 2.30. Have a flight in two hours. I so much want to hold you and I thought you would say, if not me then who? Instead, you judge me again and again. I care about you so I naturally want to be close to you.*

Mansa: *How many women have you been this close to before?*

Rajan: *Three, as I have been married before. You are very special. I really care for you. Sometimes I wonder why I even come this way. You never give me anything.*

Rajan logged off and with great difficulty, Mansa resumed her work but felt jolted. She had not expected this declaration. Another reason why she was vehemently trying to suppress her feelings for him was that she sometimes thought that he regularly chased women like her and was just passing time. But now, she felt extremely special and relaxed and felt that there was no reason to mistrust him.

They were growing closer, but every now and then, guilt, fears and doubts clouded her mind. The next day they had chatted for long, almost five hours.

Rajan: *As we cannot be together in real life and we care intensely about each other, at least we could belong together in our dreams.*

Mansa: *What are you saying? You have very American sensibilities.*

Rajan: *You will never understand how I feel about you. You are stone-hearted. Don't you feel anything for me?*

Mansa: *I do.*

Rajan: *What? Tell me what? How do you feel? Or don't you feel anything at all? Don't you ever feel like coming into my arms? Say something. Getting two words out of you is like getting water out of stones.*

Mansa: *I do.*

Rajan: *Forget it. Why do I even try? Don't you ever think about me?*

Mansa: *Yes I do. But is it not wrong to think of someone and live with someone else?*

Rajan: *Then listen; this is my imagination working. Please understand, as we can't be together in real life I thought we could be together here in our own world of dreams. A fantasy. I am married and intend staying that way. I never have and will never touch another woman. I respect both our families.*

Mansa: *Our marriages are sacrosanct. Why are you even discussing marriage? As for dreams, who has control over them? Dream whatever pleases you but why tell me all this?*

Rajan: *Because you are my dream and unless we dream together it has no meaning. I feel very strongly about you.*

Mansa: *You are so filmy. Goodnight. Bye.*

Rajan: *Bye.*

By then her office assistant had already knocked thrice to arrange her lunch, but seeing her gaze fixed on her laptop and looking very befuddled, had walked off without disturbing her.

Whenever they talked, time seemed to stop still and neither could have enough of the other. Mansa rested her head on her table and shut her eyes, reflecting on how her life had changed in the past few months. She wondered what lay in store for her in the future and where life was going. They had both tried, but had failed to walk away from each other several times.

Mansa spent the entire day entangled in the same mental

turmoil. But she found it within herself to take charge of her conclave preparations in a spirited manner. She wasn't expecting to hear from Rajan at night as he had a flight to catch. Towards the evening, feeling tremendous emotional and physical fatigue, she left her office early. These days her eyes ached and dark circles had begun to show below her eyes; she was losing her appetite and weight.

Mansa sat at the dinner table deep in thought, hunger miles away. Feeling a little under the weather, she planned to wind up the day earlier than usual. She wasn't expecting to hear from Rajan that night, but a last message check before going to sleep was her usual routine. She logged in and a note from him touched her essence.

Rajan was not online, but his message lingered in her psyche.

I was looking for you in every girl. Where were you? Maybe we are far away and can't meet, but at least we can be each other's in our dreams.

This message was enough to derail the guilt from her heart to quite an extent; she felt as though her visceral feeling for Rajan was being echoed in his sentiments towards her too. And he was her true love, who had been looking for her everywhere in every life. It reinforced the quaint feeling she had experienced every now and then that she had known him in a previous life. And the reason that she had never felt infatuated or attracted to anyone till date was because her deeper self always knew that she would meet him some day, somewhere for sure. She now recognized that her restlessness and longing for this man had always been there and now that he had arrived in her life, why should she feel guilty? She soon found justifications for her feelings; after all, it was the very first time that she was undergoing these experiences.

His words sounded as honest and truthful as her scriptures of the Ramayana and the Gita, which were the major guiding principles of her ideal Hindu way of life. Even her mind made mental adjustments citing that true love was love for God, and marriage at the end of day was a social contract, and no contract could ever be greater than the feeling of true love towards someone. After all, their family members were not involved and no one's interest was at stake. The love that Mansa felt for Rajan was pure, ethereal and transcendental. She rationalized that marriage was a socio-legal bond, not as sacred and divine as love, like the love that Radha and Krishna shared or as described in the Sufi tradition. After all, she argued with herself, she hadn't even seen him physically. So, this was the purest form of love that had ever existed.

She had worked hard to set up her business, yet she was ready to jeopardize everything for this newfound relationship. Abhimansa, which she had established with a great struggle and which had become her reason to live, did not seem important when compared to Rajan. For that matter, nothing else seemed important in comparison to him. She felt magically charmed by his free-spirited, flirtatious manner. He lived on the other side of the globe, yet he occupied a great deal of her mental space.'

For Mansa, chatting with him was the kind of stuff that dreams were made of. And she felt lucky to be living this dream. Rajan was slowly getting more and more vocal about his feelings, while she could feel herself becoming more and more receptive.

The next day as they were having a romantic chat, Rajan wrote: Sunte hain ki mil jaati hai hur cheez dua se. (I have heard one gets everything upon praying [for it])

Mansa gazed dreamily at her screen and typed: *Oh it's a beautiful line, why don't you complete it?*

Rajan: *I deliberately left it incomplete...*

Mansa: *Why? Please complete it.*

Rajan: Ek din tujhe bhi maang ke dekhenge khuda se. (*Some day, I will ask for you too from Almighty.*)

Mansa: *Oh, such beautiful lines.*

Rajan: *Not more beautiful than you. Ilu Ilu.*

Mansa: *What?*

Rajan: *Joking.*

Mansa: *Hmm*

Rajan: *ILU.*

Her heart was beating faster than ever and senses were numb. She had never expected to hear someone say 'I love you' to her in her lifetime.

She was beginning to feel a sense of estrangement from Abhijit, to the extent that she even began avoiding his touch sometimes. The stranger's words always rang in her ears: 'Being married doesn't mean we are dead. Married people can develop feelings too.'

9

Culinary Spice

> 'No, this trick won't work… How on earth are you ever going
> to explain in terms of chemistry and physics so important a
> biological phenomenon as first love?'
>
> —Albert Einstein

AUTUMN WAS FAST approaching. It is a time when New Delhi
gets a new lease of life after the brutal heat and begins to
be livelier. Plays, theatre, musical events, drama, ballet, food
festivals, movie festivals, cultural events, or any other even
would spring up everywhere. Mansa's life was following a
parallel too. It was as though a pleasant season was about to
sprout in Mansa's life too.

Since time immemorial, the city of Delhi has been a
melting pot of religions, cultures and ideas from different parts
of the world. One can feel the fervour and flavour of Delhi
peaking most intensely from October to February, as the city's

miscellaneous millions celebrate festivals and events like 'Phool Wallon Ki Sair' to the Suraj Kund Mela with zeal and zest.

Mansa's entire team was also working with a similar ardour to make their forthcoming, first international event a big success. It was to be an International Culinary Conclave to launch fresh ideas in nutritive cooking. Her hard work of previous years had paid rich dividends despite operating from a modest office. She had succeeded in penetrating the upmarket niche clientele of Delhi and had started becoming known in the gourmet circles. Her professional association with her mentor, Gary Om, Pratap and the other cooking course batchmates had been immensely fortuitous. On her pay roll were a dietician, a nutritionist and a chef, who churned out recipes with Mansa at the helm of affairs. They conducted seminars and workshops to create awareness of the importance of healthy, nutritious and delicious vegetarian cuisine. As it was a concept created and promoted by her, Mansa was being touted as a new vegan gourmet guru in Delhi, and some of the corporates, designer restaurants and five-star hotels were happy to support her cause and cooperate with her. Albeit a late starter in life, she had come a long way in a very short time due to her innovative approach, pleasant interpersonal skills, honesty and hard work.

The Taj Hotel was the official host for the upcoming conclave and besides Gary Om and other delegates, Mansa was going to be one of the key speakers at the event which was a great honour for her. Mansa always thought that since they stood for health, style and taste, it was of paramount importance that she herself should be a living symbol of a healthy lifestyle including style, simplicity and grace.

These days, she was working particularly hard to come up with pioneering food concepts to share with other delegates in her upcoming conclave on 'Spices and Gourmet Cuisines'. The conclave was being promoted as one of the biggest events of the year in the food industry by Tushita.

Mansa felt good about herself, her special person online and the high from the conclave made her feel on cloud nine. She was finally focusing on her conclave with a renewed gusto. It was now just ten days to her event. Just the other night, she had chatted till late with Rajan, who had kept cajoling her with poetry and his humorous 'talk about nothing'.

During the past few months, Mansa had spent so much time chatting online with Rajan that she had lost touch with real people and many good friends. While preparing to sleep, she recounted how much Pratap had supported her in the beginning, how she had been typically rigid and hadn't even accepted his offer for a lunch or coffee. Pratap being Pratap, a thorough gentleman, had never asked her again since he understood and respected Mansa's conservative attitude.

The next day, when Abhijit came back home, he gave Mansa some news that completely enraptured her. Abhijit was going to go to London and then to Switzerland for official business, and wanted Mansa to join him. An opportunity to spend extra time with Malvika always excited Mansa. But this time around, there was another reason why she couldn't stop grinning. It sounded too good to be true, as only during her last chat, Rajan had shared that he had an impending official trip to Europe. She had never thought even in her wildest dreams that she would get an opportunity to meet him so early. He hardly ever came to India and although she had travelled to the US a few times, she had never been to the West Coast. So, she felt it was providential that the timing of her trip was to coincide with his visit to Europe.

She found it hard to wait for the morning to break the news to Rajan, as she did not find the opportunity to log in from home or even message him at night. She had hardly slept at night and it was soon morning. She had half a mind to skip her morning run, as there was so much to do, but she thought that now she would have to be extra careful about her looks and weight. After all, she was going to see that someone special for the first and maybe the last time for all she knew.

She walked mechanically into the bathroom and removed her nightie to slip into a pair of shorts and a T-shirt. She didn't forget to take her headphones along. These days, she downloaded all the songs and ghazals that Rajan sent her and played them whenever she had any free time.

Because of him, she was also rediscovering her lost love for poetry and ghazals, which she had given up as soon as she had married Abhijit, as he was quite averse to the objectification of women in any form. Till a few months ago, for the last twenty years, she had not even thought about ghazals and poetry. She had given herself completely to domesticity without ever being conscious of doing it. But Rajan had brought back her fondness for music and now, every minute she wanted more and more of it, regretting giving it up.

In a sleepy state, she put on her earphones. A Sufi ghazal sent by Rajan began to play and she started jogging. She had barely jogged for a few metres, when she suddenly stumbled, falling down with a heavy thud on the rough rocky terrain close to the golf course. She somehow got up and attracted the attention of some fellow joggers, who offered to help her to a nearby public washroom, suggesting that she go back home. She ignored their advice, as she wanted to complete her designated amount of exercise for the day.

As soon as she reached home, Shonali, Abhijit and Bela stared at her in dismay.

'Oh my God! What happened to you?' Abhijit exclaimed.

Without replying, Mansa ran to a mirror. She looked at her contorted features and bruised and bleeding skin disbelievingly. The only worry on her mind was that she would have to see Rajan for the first time with scars on her face.

Abhijit came up behind her and said, 'Come on. Let's go to the doctor without any delay.'

Mansa stubbornly ignored everyone. All of Abhijit's advice and concern fell on deaf ears, as she had already made up her mind to attend office as usual. She carefully took a quick shower, the streams of refreshing water causing her more pain, as she inspected her body closely with her eyes and hands. Instead of feeling worried about her injuries, she felt proud of her flat belly. Standing erect, she could feel the stream of water flowing between her breasts down to the more erogenous parts of her body. She had read somewhere that when a woman stands straight and looking down can see her vagina, it means she is shapely. Right now, that was the kick that Mansa was feeling. Suddenly she became aware of someone banging on the bathroom door, and the sensation of pain returned.

When she came out, Abhijit was ready to take her to the

doctor. 'Come on, you are not going to office today,' he said.

Mansa retorted agitatedly and stubbornly, 'I have to go to a conference before office, which is most important. And I am the best judge of whether I need a doctor at all.'

Abhijit pleaded, 'Work is not going to suffer. Look at you, you are badly injured!'

Shonali agreed with her father. 'Please listen to Papa and go to the doctor first, Mom!'

But Mansa adamantly ignored everyone. She popped a painkiller, applied ointment, and covered the rest of her face with sunscreen. She patted on a light layer of foundation along with lip gloss and without eating breakfast, went out. As she scampered up the steps of the convention centre, she felt self-conscious, as many eyes moved in her direction. It was certainly not out of admiration, but shock, as no normal person in such a state would have stepped out of the house. She quietly entered the convention hall through the back door and took her seat in the last row.

After the fourth speaker finished, they dispersed for coffee. As she went to the coffee lobby looking for familiar faces, she was greeted by a stranger. Before she could exchange pleasantries, the lady popped a question, 'Are you a victim of domestic violence?'

Despite being in a considerable amount of pain, Mansa burst out laughing. Her mind conjured up images of her gentle husband, who had not so much even raised his voice at her, whatever the provocation. At the same time she thought how easy it was for people in this busy bustling city to notice someone's external wounds, but how only a few could actually look at what was within.

Once she had even asked him: *Why don't you upload a photograph of yours?*

And a flat reply had come from Rajan: *No, I don't like the way I look these days.*

His looks did not matter to Mansa, as she was more attracted to his mind and his soul.

She barely had a few days between her conclave and her night flight to Europe. When she reached office, it was almost late afternoon and she thought that she had already missed her talking time with Rajan. Slowing down and taking stock of her injuries, she mentally went through her usual to-do list. As she went online, she did what she always did mechanically and saw the green smiling dot although it was pretty late. She was excited about sharing her happiness about her impending trip to Europe coinciding with his trip. She also wanted to tell him about her fall, and how and why it had happened.

Mansa: *While listening to your Sufi song and thinking of you, I had a bad fall today as I was jogging.*

Rajan didn't pay much attention to what she said or even understand the enormity of the fall. She also did not touch upon it again.

She typed, choking with emotion, her fingers trembling: *Rajan, were you serious that day when you said, that I am the only person you prayed to God for or were you just reciting poetry?*

Rajan: *I never say things that I don't mean.*

Mansa: *Then your wish is granted. I am coming to Europe at the same time as you. Oh my God, aren't you excited? Is it not God's magic? The moment you wished it, God arranged for us to meet. Because your prayer was sincere, true to the core. It came from the depth of your soul.*

Rajan: *What do you mean?*

Mansa: *I mean is it not a great divine mystical coincidence that we will be in Europe at the same time? I want to see all the places that you have frequented, especially LBS. All of your favourite spots, everything that you ever touched or liked, everywhere that you have been, and it will give me a true feeling of being with you in those moments when you were there.*

Rajan then went about giving her tips on local cuisines and exotic fare. From shopping to restaurants to scenic spots to tourist spots to farmer's market, he guided her with all the information he had. They talked and talked, till he felt sleepy.

10

A Weird Trance

'Then, we met, and everything changed, the cynic has become the converted, the sceptic, an ardent zealot.'

—E.A. Bucchianeri

MANSA WAS THANKFUL for the coming weekend, as she thought she could catch some rest and tend to her wounds. She would also be able to devote more time and energy to her conclave preparation. For Saturday, Mansa had fixed a meeting with Tushita at home to discuss certain media- and PR-related issues for the conclave.

Tushita arrived at the scheduled time. This was Tushita's first visit to Bhargav House after their culinary course a couple of years back. While waiting in the drawing room, her gaze was attracted by a picture of Mansa and her husband and she commented just as Mansa entered the room, 'You two are soulmates!'

The words sounded alien to Mansa's ears, as she was only physically present at home these days, her mind often wandering to the cyber world she found more meaningful. When her gaze fell on Mansa, Tushita cried out, 'Oh my God! How did you manage to hurt yourself so badly?'

Mansa told her and Tushita commented, 'Oh dear! You have had a karmic fall.'

Mansa narrowed her eyebrows. 'What? What is that supposed to mean?' She wondered if it was an unintended reference to some impending catastrophe. 'We all fall down some time or the other. Now what is this new business of a karmic fall?' Mansa questioned.

'Today is not the day for karmic discussions. I am here for another purpose. Let's take care of that first,' said Tushita.

Tushita was long gone after their discussion, but had left behind ripples in Mansa's already turbulent mind. 'Soulmates!' Mansa scoffed. She now baulked at the idea of Abhijit being her soulmate. The meeting had concluded on an optimistic note, as Tushita had shared her strategy to optimize media involvement with their current venture. But her mind was flooded by the 'karmic fall'.

Tushita had offered to give the facial wound a healing. It was a large crisscross patch of very tender pink skin on her forehead just below the bump and above her eyebrow. Stereotypically, Mansa's first reaction would have been, 'What nonsense!' Instead, she had heard herself say, 'Really? Will that really work?'

In any case, she thought, she had nothing to lose. All she wanted was to get rid of all these scars before she met Rajan for first time. She was desperate to look her best when she met him in Europe and she also wanted to look presentable for the conclave. As she settled in the position following Tushita's directions with her eyes shut, she felt a soothing warmth envelope her wound. After about two minutes, when Tushita asked her to open her eyes, it was as though she had come out of a trance. Tushita nudged her to go and check her wound in a mirror, and to her utter disbelief, Mansa had found the scars healed.

Sunday gave her somewhat more respite, as she spent time just pottering around at home. She knelt beside a side table to straighten the crease of a runner, and gaped at her big black eye in a photo frame's reflection. Again, while absentmindedly looking at her and Abhijit's photograph, Tushita's mention of the karmic fall crossed her mind. Suppressing an eerie feeling that was forming deep within her, she smiled wryly as she looked at the painful bruises reflected in the photo frame's glass front.

Her right toe had turned completely blue. The left knee was badly bruised and the right elbow still hurt due to internal swelling, as she had unsuccessfully tried preventing the face-down fall by balancing herself on it. Even her lower lip was swollen and it hurt to smile. Yet, a naughty smile lingered on her disfigured features. Tushita had implied that the fall was the outcome of some wrong karma, which should not have been committed. It also signified a fall and injury were imminent because of the direction in which her interpersonal relationships were heading.

As she went about the day smiling to herself, her thoughts

were frequently interrupted by echoes of 'soulmates', 'karmic fall' and Tushita's firm belief that all worries and problems of the present life and the people who cross our path in this life are connected to our past-life karma. She strongly suggested that Mansa should try holistic healing for her migraine and maybe it could also cure Abhijit's of his recurrent childhood dream of being pushed from a bus when he wants to board it.

Tushita held the belief that where medical science fails, past-life regression therapy helps. She had poured the ideas of PLR, soul healing and crystal therapy into Mansa's ears. The sceptic in her mind scorned at all this, while her heart wondered if the cure for Abhijit's recurring nightmare and her childhood migraines lay in holistic healing, then what was the harm in trying it once as an experiment? Yet she knew she could never convince Abhijit of its efficacy, although for the first time, she had actually experienced alternate healing when her wound had instantly dried up. However, knowing Abhijit's views and rigidity on irrationality and any lack of logic, her thoughts about convincing him were fleeting. Even in the past, any suggestion to treat her migraines and his nightmares with alternate therapy had ended with strong resistance and ridicule from him.

A name—Rajan—had always rested deep down in her soul in her subconscious mind, and this was probably one reason that she had drifted into a relationship with this man on the internet despite all her prudence, reservations and resistance. She had always experienced a connection with the name Rajan, but she had no words to articulate how she felt drawn to the name and the bearer of the name. Everyone is entitled to their own analysis and philosophy of life, Mansa thought. She herself had always been cynical about the idea of past lives. And yet, she couldn't deny how she had felt drawn to this name in some subliminal manner and the reason could be that she had known someone by this name in a past life.

On Thursday, one of the biggest challenges of Mansa's professional life was coming up for which she had been preparing for a few months. Coupled with that was the challenge of managing to look presentable, what with her facial landscape being discoloured and covered with injuries.

In two days' time, Abhijit was to leave for London for his upcoming conference. This also meant that Abhijit would not be around during the most testing moment of her life. She decided to have a run through of her entire event before his departure. She valued Abhijit's advice so much even though hospitality was not his field. Contrary to what she would have done in earlier days, she hadn't turned down the opportunity of hosting a conclave in Abhijit's absence.

Besides the stress of organizing and participating in an event of such magnitude for the first time, there was also the stress of joining Abhijit in London the next day after the conference. As she was going to Europe, there was shopping to take care of. As usual, Malvika had a long list of what she wanted her mom to bring to London, even though she visited India twice a year. What compounded the situation was her emotional volatility due to Rajan's growing demands for intimacy, which troubled Mansa's conservative nature. Despite this, even with the mounting pressures and heavy work schedule, she was not willing to sacrifice her chat time.

Days passed quickly. Abhijit left for London on Monday night. D-day arrived and went smoothly and successfully. As Mansa left for London the very next day, she missed the media buzz her event created. The day she was leaving, shopping and packing were to be taken care of. Exhausted from the previous day's event, Mansa woke up a little late and gave the morning gym a miss, since she had to organize her household for Shonali who would be left behind. Mansa was nervous about leaving Shonali behind for such a long time, but she did not want her daughters to be like she had been. She wanted her daughters to be assertive and financially independent.

Before packing, she had to comply with Malvika's long shopping list and also buy stuff that Shonali would need. Household needs had to be inspected in micro detail. Shopping, packing, giving instructions and an urge to spend more time with Shonali had given Mansa negligible time to chat with Rajan during the last two days.

The next thing she knew, it was time to alight at Heathrow.

11

31 Miles

> '*Sometimes the things that are felt the most are expressed between two souls over the distance and over time... where no words abide.*'
>
> —C. Joybell C.

AS MANSA DESCENDED from the aircraft, a cool chill and a very bright day greeted her. The feel and experience of London was like never before. The warm glow of the sunshine and coming proximity to her online stranger made her feel exhilarated. In her mental state for the past few months, Abhijit was the last person on her mind and all she could think about was Rajan. As her cell phone came to life, she received a message from Abhijit saying that she would find his cab driver waiting for her at the airport, but Malu at the moment was not in London. Deep within, she longed for a message from Rajan. Not finding one from him deeply disappointed her. Now she was in an unusual hurry to reach her hotel room, not to embrace Abhijit, but to catch up with Rajan.

Her happiness had known no bounds when Rajan had told her that he was scheduled for a work-cum-vacation to the Swiss Alps around the same time that she and Abhijit would be there and would be visiting London and Paris too. Trusting blindly in everything he had ever told her, she believed that he had conceived and planned the entire programme in a manner so that they could meet.

When she reached her room, she found that Abhijit had already eaten his breakfast and was waiting for her even though he was getting late. His conference was scheduled on all weekdays from 9.30 a.m. to 5 p.m. in the same hotel where they were staying. He welcomed her with an embrace and quickly left. Mansa didn't mind him leaving her behind so quickly at all. She quickly unzipped her bag and rang the reception for the Wi-Fi log in details. She was elated to find Rajan online. He was going to Paris almost the same time as Mansa and Abhijit. Instead of continuing to chat, she climbed up on the bed and began to jump in joy. After a few hops, she caught her reflection in the full-length mirror in the room and blushed. She had never behaved so unconventionally before.

The beauty of London from her room suddenly seemed more picturesque. The very thought that she was staying near the business school he had graduated from gave her enormous pleasure. She wanted to visit every nook and corner he had been in, all his favourite joints, restaurants, streets. She was bursting with happiness and the urge to discover more about him overwhelmed her.

Online, Rajan left a message that he wanted to take her on a guided tour of his alma mater city online.

Mansa: *Tell me; tell me please, all about your favourite places.*

Rajan: *Go and explore the place yourself; we can always chat later when you go back to India.*

He told her about his favourite coffee shop and other places of interest to him, sounding keyed up while narrating incidents from his time there. At the end of their chat, even though tired, Mansa decided it would be wise not to sleep. She quickly brushed her teeth and realized how hungry she was. She hadn't eaten anything during the flight.

Brimming with happiness, she explored the refrigerator and zeroed down on an apple and a pack of corn chips. She downed everything with a huge mug of cappuccino, as she relived an August conversation with Rajan for the umpteenth time. He had quoted from a great Persian poet.

Rajan: *Prayers have the power to bring you anything.*

Mansa: *Beautiful line.*

Rajan: *Not more beautiful than you.*

Mansa: *But why didn't you complete it?*

Rajan: *I deliberately left it.*

Mansa: *Why?*

Rajan: *If it is true then I want to ask for you, you and only you.*

Mansa had blushed and hadn't known how to respond. That night, she had slept with a smile and belief in the truth of whatever Rajan had uttered. It had sounded so divine, so pure. It was enough to drive a balanced and controlled creature like her insane. And now she was so close to meeting him.

Completely entrenched in her thoughts, before leaving for Europe, she had coaxed an unsuspecting Abhijit to alter his programme to gain an extra day in Switzerland to coincide with Rajan's visit. She had felt manipulative, but at that point in time, meeting Rajan prevailed over all the goodness she was worth.

Equipped with all this new information, inspiring her to explore London via a new set of eyes, Mansa was keen on using local transport to get a better feel of the place. Days before leaving for London Mansa had informed Madhulika, her childhood friend, that she would be in London. To add to her delight Madhulika had called her as soon as she had arrived in London. She had always bonded very well with Madhulika. Her eyes felt moist as she thought of how she had let her friend down during her hour of a crisis. And the realization of what she had done to her friend had come so late in her life, through Rajan. She wondered if destiny and karma always followed a charted path.

Madhulika had gleefully agreed to accompany her in exploring London as though they were still grad students of the late 1980s. Madhulika came to Mansa's hotel and left her car there.

Mansa and Madhulika had been very close in their growing up senior school years and had spent most of their free time together chatting till late at night, watching movies on VCRs in either of their houses. They would frequent the neighbourhood Khan Market and Nirula's for an evening ice cream together. Madhulika was the only one she would step outside of her home with. Their mothers (now both dead) had been friends and neighbours for a number of years. Madhulika fell into a relationship with a classmate as soon as she joined college. Consequently, the time she spent with Mansa became sparse. And when they were in their final year, one summer afternoon as Mansa returned from her college, she saw a lot of commotion in her house. Madhulika's mom was there with a relative and was sobbing as she sat next to her mother.

Mansa couldn't believe what she heard next. Madhulika's mother said, 'Madhu hasn't come home since yesterday. Most of her friends are saying that she is with Sandeep and if it's true, her dad is going to kill them both. He is mad with rage. I want to talk to Mansa. I am sure she knows everything. It's not possible that Madhu would have kept Mansa in dark.'

Mansa had received a double blow. One came from the fact that her closest friend hadn't confided in her—what kind of a friendship was this? And the second blow was that her friend, almost an ideal in her eyes, could do such a contemptible thing as running away with a guy. It horrified and repulsed her that Madhulika, of all girls, had done it.

The same evening she received a phone call from Madhulika, saying that she had married Sandeep and left Delhi to live in Chandigarh so that she couldn't be tracked. Madhulika's parents called Mansa in the evening and instead of supporting her friend, she had sung in one voice with them, saying that an immoral act had been done by Madhulika and had brought shame upon the family. Mansa and Madhulika had lost touch since then for many number of years. Since her association with Rajan she had deeply regretted her past behaviour towards Madhulika and even empathized with how passions can play on a person in love. Deep down in her heart,

Mansa felt guilty that when Madhulika eloped to marry her schooltime boyfriend Sandeep, and needed her support, she had sided with Madhulika's father and was quick to make moral judgements against Madhulika. She wanted to apologize to Madhulika for her past behaviour and her stubbornness in not being able to forgive Madhulika for what she did to her parents over twenty years ago. Having made this resolve, she now felt so much lighter.

Mansa had already made a mental list of all of Rajan's regular haunts from his college days. She had been to London a few times before, but those trips had been confined to top London attractions such as London Eye, Big Ben, Natural History Museum and Buckingham Palace. Rajan's list of London favourites was nothing very unusual, but she wanted to explore London through his eyes.

His list consisted of: Jake's Burger Bar, Canary Wharf Underground Station, Floating Chinese Restaurant on the Grand Union Canal near Regent's Park, London Business School, London Tower Bridge, Canary Wharf Farmer's Market, and Taylor St Barista's for coffee. And of course, Big Ben, which she had already seen before.

Mansa's girls and Madhulika's boys were about the same age and good friends too. Malvika often visited Madhulika during her short breaks whenever she did not visit India. As they drifted towards the tube station, Madhulika said, 'Malvika is on a cruise trip for five days away from London with her friends which she did not want to miss. It was a last minute programme and she couldn't inform you so I told her that I would explain it all to you. I hope you are okay with it.'

Mansa said, 'Yes of course. Why should she not enjoy her college life with her friends?' Strangely enough, Mansa had not felt a mother's disappointment when she did not find her daughter there at once when she reached London.

Madhulika said happily, 'That's great—you are such an understanding mother. Now you have a few days before you meet Malvika.'

Mansa said hesitantly: 'Madhu, I want to say something. Please forgive me for me being such a terrible friend and giving you no support when you needed me the most.'

Madhulika was surprised, 'What are you talking about?'

Mansa, with a penitent smile, said, 'You know what I am talking about. We should have talked about it years ago. Please say that I am forgiven.'

Madhulika, with her usual hearty laughter, said, 'Mana, I am not sure what are you talking about but whatever it is you are forgiven, forgiven, forgiven.'

Mansa went on, 'But I am serious. I was never supposed to judge you as a friend but I did. Madhu, I am talking about the time when you married Sandeep and I sided with your dad.'

Madhulika replied, 'It's long forgotten and forgiven. I know you wished me well and feared for my safety.'

Mansa was not sure whether she was smiling or crying at her friend's understanding and warmth. She gently squeezed Madhulika's hand in acknowledgement of the reprieve granted by her friend.

Madhulika asked her, 'Where do you want to go first?'

Mansa replied, 'Let's start with London Business School.'

Madhulika asked with a twinkle in her eyes, 'London

Business School? Oh yes! You could still go to a business school if you like. Unlike back home, here colleges do cater to all age groups, unless you are thinking about your daughters.'

Mansa said naughtily, 'No, I am planning to earn a degree for myself. Have no CV, no job, no career and no life. And maybe I can deceive myself that I can get away with looking like a student and enjoy campus life once again. Why not? What's the harm?'

They both giggled as the lift stopped at the tube level from where they had to board the train. When they reached the campus, Mansa was surprised at the happiness the sight of the London Business School gave her, except for the mystical attraction she had always felt towards this business school and the name Rajan. Even when she had first accepted his friend request she had felt that she had known that this person existed somewhere. There was something mysteriously familiar and paranormal about his existence. It was as though the name rang a bell somewhere in the deep recesses of her mind.

Her euphoria had reached its peak, and suddenly triggered grief; she felt that she should have been on the campus with Rajan. She wished intensely that they had met when younger and had dated. Then they would have been here together. She missed him more than ever.

Mansa and Madhulika walked around the campus, stopping for coffee at Rajan's suggested places. As the day dissolved into night, they decided to settle for a very late lunch at the floating Chinese restaurant. The serene magic of the place made her thank Rajan for his choice of place and yet again prompted her to get to her room quickly to catch up with him. Once back in her room, she enthusiastically detailed all the information to Rajan although she did not see him online. Late in the evening, as Abhijit entered the room, he was in a rush to clasp her in his arms. Abhijit did not notice, but her complete lack of interest in him surprised Mansa.

Abhijit asked her if she wanted to go out for dinner, but her hectic past few days and morning adventures prompted her to say no. They finally decided in favour of a quick bite in their own room and to sleep early.

As the sun filtered through the drapes, Mansa lazily opened her eyes and got up with a jerk, as she noticed a tall handsome figure moving about the room in a formal navy blue suit and grey tie. It was 8.30 a.m. She had slept for really long. She couldn't help but smile at the perfect symmetry of Abhijit's features. His sharp nose and angular jawline always made him stand apart in a crowd. She remembered how friends had complimented her on his great looks, which she had hardly noticed when they were to be married. Today after so many years she realized what her friends must see when they looked at him; she was viewing him from another woman's perspective, because these days she was mentally always with Rajan.

Abhijit turned towards her with a warm smile and asked, 'Mana, should I fix you tea or you will do it yourself? I am already running late for the conference.'

Mansa stretched out and said lazily, 'Please, Abhi, tea. You know I can't get up till someone hands over my tea.'

Abhijit obliged lovingly and Mansa slipped again beneath the covers. She experienced twinges of guilt while Abhijit made her tea, as she thought of the double decker hop on/hop off tour that she was going to take to see the city through Rajan's eyes. But the guilt only lasted while Abhijit was in the room. Once he left, she ran for her laptop. To her delight, she saw the green dot.

She mentally consolidated the places she had not seen. She filled in Rajan on the places she was planning to cover—Jake's Burger Bar, Canary Wharf and Farmer's Market. Today she was by herself, as Madhulika could not join her because she had work to do. Mansa didn't mind being left to herself to explore, as she cherished the feeling of being closer to Rajan in his city of educational redemption.

As she hopped onto the Redline, her first destination was the Farmer's Market, as Rajan had fervently told her to go there in the early morning hours, especially on a Sunday. Even though it was a Friday, it was a treat for the senses. Everywhere she looked, there were stalls selling silver trinkets, homemade chocolates, ice candy, cheese, fresh vegetables and fruits, jams, jellies, pickles, among other items. It reminded her of haats in Indian villages, which she had seen from a distance while travelling on highways.

The fresh aroma of various kinds of cheese, bread, marmalades and various baked and fried snacks made their way to her nose, but her eyes explored every Indian male face earnestly. She had a strong belief that today, come what may, Rajan would pop up from somewhere to meet her.

While sipping Rajan-recommended coffee, she found herself staring at the men walking into the coffee shop, although she had a very faint idea of Rajan's build and physical disposition. She had seen just a childhood photograph of his. She had a vague mental picture of him, which exactly matched the one she had had in her subconscious mind since youth. By now her hopes were falling flat. Leave aside his physical presence; she had not received even a call or a tiny SMS. It looked like a meeting was not going to happen today.

Dejectedly, she decided to head to Jake's Burger Bar via Canary Wharf. She hadn't eaten lunch. As she entered the burger joint, it was almost 4 p.m., almost the time Abhijit had promised to meet her there. After hopping on and off for most of the day, an otherwise pleasant and upbeat day was moving towards a gloomy and disappointing end. She again wondered how many women Rajan might have had relationships with. She remembered how she was brave enough to ask him: How many women have you felt this close to before?

Rajan: *Three, as I have been married before and there was another one whose heart I broke.*

She had found it hard to believe him. Nevertheless, his reply had made her feel very special. He sounded so romantic, charming, and even well-rehearsed in his art of wooing women. Sometimes she felt that she was making a fool of herself, but she couldn't care less.

She had barely settled down, when she saw a handsome, smiling face emerge from the far end of the bar, heading speedily towards her. Abhijit always tried his best to never keep her waiting. Abhijit seated himself beside her and with a warm smile asked her, 'Why are you looking so pale?'

Mansa said, 'It's probably the trip and exhaustion after organizing the conclave combined.'

Abhijit exclaimed, 'But you looked so fresh and cheerful

in the morning!'

'Then probably it is the accumulated effect of hopping on and off buses the whole day.' With a smile, she tried shifting the topic to Abhijit's conference, but she knew he would have none of it.

Abhijit was concerned as they were to travel to Switzerland the next morning. 'If you want, we could cruise the city some more and shop a bit right now or we can spend time in the room.'

Feeling utterly selfish, Mansa decided to treat Abhijit warmly and said, 'You take the call. I'm okay with either option.' Hiding her disappointment, she let her hand slip into Abhijit's hand and they both glided in a car towards London Tower Bridge.

It was almost 10 p.m. when they entered their room after dinner and Abhijit seemed in an unusual rush to pin her down under him. He didn't even let her change, completely overpowering her. Mansa, briefly and unsuccessfully, tried putting Rajan at the back of her mind and feeling sorry for Abhijit, gently stroked and caressed the back of his head. Abhijit chanted, 'Mana, Mana,' and buried himself deep inside her.

The next morning, she woke up and gingerly caressed Abhijit's back. He was still entwined around her. When she stirred, he opened his eyes and gave her another warm hug.

'Don't spend too much time in bed with your tea; we have a train to catch to Geneva. Are we going to catch or miss the train?' Abhijit asked Mansa teasingly.

Deep down, Mansa realized how unfair she was being to this man, who could not look or think beyond his family's happiness. She didn't understand why all his goodness, love and kind gestures were being weighed down under her urge to connect with Raj, as she was beginning to call Rajan in their romantic moments.

She felt a deep unhappiness coupled with a trickle of hope. He was quite far from her, yet she had built so many castles in the air. And not even a week of her month-long trip had passed. She cherished the thought that they would be in Geneva soon, where she and Rajan would be spatially so close that there could be no reason not to meet. The very thought increased her pulse rate. Abhijit's second reminder brought her back to her senses. He was right, if they had to catch the early morning Euro Star via Paris, she had barely fifteen or twenty minutes to get dressed. The very next moment, she threw her body into action at the speed of light. By the time she got down to the lobby in fitted blue denims and a snug pale pink top, Abhijit had already completed the checkout formalities and had a cab waiting. She had no time to even look at the tempting buffet spread. She quickly grabbed a fruit and matched Abhijit's pace to get into the waiting car. She considered herself lucky when they made it to the train on time. She was lucky again, when after about half an hour, they were served a nice meal of their choice on the way.

Mansa noticed there were not many people in the coach in sharp contrast to the multitudes one comes across in Indian trains and at Indian railway stations. All the varied aromas, vendors, stalls, kiosks, noises, mayhem, stray dogs, and most of all, the sea of humanity one witnesses at Indian railway stations were all conspicuous by their absence.

Abundant green fields extended on both sides of the track along with ceaseless stretches of sparkling water, gleaming sunshine, fluffy clouds and lazy hillocks. An hour passed quickly, as they moved closer to Paris. Mansa's hope and excitement were beginning to soar again. She was inching closer to her dream of seeing Rajan in reality. At the Paris station, they lugged their respective cases and as they changed trains, she couldn't help but feel in awe of the fresh air and the lack of crowds.

Once seated inside, she realized they were the only people in the compartment. She stretched out her legs and rested her head on Abhijit's shoulder. As always, Abhijit had offered her the seat of her choice and made sure of her utmost comfort. They had barely been seated when a ticket checker walked in and stated, 'Oh, this is executive class. Do you have valid tickets?' His tone and manner were resentful and derogatory. As Abhijit produced the tickets from his pocket, Mansa struggled to contain her irritation. Though she had heard of such things happening to Indians sometimes, she had never experienced this kind of slight before.

She decided to concentrate on better things and was quickly captivated by the panoramic view of the Alps as the train whizzed towards Geneva. Mansa again reminded herself that she must not forget to pick some wine, chocolates and cheese before they left as these days all she thought about was Rajan.

Soon, they were disembarking at Geneva. Mansa again found herself overcome by a desire to be all by herself in the hotel room so she could go online and connect with Rajan. En route their hotel, Abhijit asked, 'Are you feeling fresh enough to do some sightseeing right now or do you want to head to the hotel first?'

She already had a readymade answer, 'I want to take a short nap, Abhi, if you don't mind.' She very well knew that once in bed, Abhijit would not be up for at least a few hours and she would have all the time in the world to connect with Rajan. Her plan worked. Once on the bed, Abhijit fell into a deep sleep and to her good fortune, Rajan immediately came online too. He was to reach Switzerland after two days on the coming Monday. And on the weekend, she was scheduled to leave for London to spend the rest of her time with her daughter. She had three full days with Rajan. It was Malvika's idea that they should reach London on the weekend so that she could spend her weekend with her parents.

Rajan's unending trail of love messages kept Mansa glued to her laptop. He repeatedly said that he loved her, was crazy about her, and couldn't think about anything except her. Her hands felt hot and her cheeks flushed. She wondered what would happen if they met. From a distance, she could see her new Bebe tracks and jacket, which she had just picked up in London while thinking of Rajan. The pale white track bottoms teamed with the red and cream fitted jacket would enhance her figure and beauty, thought Mansa. She was dying to wear them before Rajan. He appeared to be longing to see her.

Finally Mansa patronizingly agreed: *All right, why don't you join me for a morning walk here? Is it too far from where you will be staying?*

To her disbelief, her message was followed by a long silence, leaving her confounded.

Finally, Rajan asked: *Where are you staying?*

Mansa replied: *Geneva Sheraton*

Rajan: *Yes, it is really very far from where I will be staying. And why should I come to Karol Bagh Sheraton? Have you come to meet me, and only me? Why should I come and meet you? Have you come alone?*

Mansa, in shocked dismay, typed: *Who would let me come alone so far? My husband is here. We are here on a business-cum-vacation trip just the way you are.*

Rajan: *Are you a queen or something that I should come and see you? Maybe I would have thought a little differently if you had come alone.*

For a moment, Mansa thought that he was pulling her leg. She wondered why he had referred to her hotel as 'Karol Bagh Sheraton'.

Nevertheless, she ignored her embarrassment and mustered the courage to type: *In the mornings I jog alone as Abhijit is not a morning person.*

But even if it was a joke, his comment had badly upset and saddened her. She had come here with such delight, hope and enthusiasm; her heart did not want to entertain even the faint possibility of not being able to see him.

Rajan: *I am busy with other things at that time. Can't come.*

Mansa was left incredibly hurt and speechless. He was the very reason why she had manipulated Abhijit into changing their dates to overlap with Rajan's. With him she had undergone a soul experience, which she had always believed existed only in fantasy. It had propelled her to travel across continents and oceans to have a glimpse of the man she had thought of day and night for several months now, whose fervent repertoire of prose and poetry had created this insanity in her, leading her to believe in an emotion she had never felt till she had met him online.

She did not quite understand what had happened now. A person who loved so much and spoke of tender emotions suddenly sounded cold and distant. Had she read or understood something which had not been said? She decided to revisit their entire conversation at night, although each word was etched very prominently in her memory.

Suddenly, feeling Abhijit turn in bed, she quickly logged out. She ran straight to the bathroom, shutting the door tight behind her. She felt heavy with fear and grief, controlling a loud sob with a great effort as she sank to the floor. She suddenly felt queasy. She thought of Abhijit's unquestioned love for her even though he had never said those three tender words to her. Even when she had asked him to say them in their most intimate moments, he had refused, calling them dramatic and hollow. Although he had never uttered 'I love you' to her in the conventional way, she knew that his every breath was dedicated to her. His care and concern were unparalleled, so much so that she had at times felt smothered.

And here she stood, divided into two equal halves. On one side was a man who had quoted poetry to express his love— had he not meant any of it? And then there was Abhijit, who could not bring himself to say those three clichéd yet magical words despite fervently loving her in his own way.

Not realizing how much time had passed, a knock on the door brought her back to life. She took a deep breath and decided to control her emotions. Quickly pacing towards the basin, she sprinkled water on her face and gave herself a shake. She looked into the mirror and smiled, trying to hide her hurt and pain. She came out to find Abhijit looking concerned, but she reassured him that she was fine.

In the morning, Abhijit changed into a white T-shirt and they reached for the door without a word or even a glance at each other. Mansa looked at Abhijit as the lift descended towards the lobby. As always, he appeared carefree. Unpretentious and unassuming, the kind soul did not even realize the torrent of emotions Mansa was going through. This was one trait she had come to find most irritating in Abhijit. She could almost never get him to look at her. Whenever they were in a gathering and she wanted to communicate with him through her eyes, he would almost never look towards her, even when she stared hard at him to gain his attention. She had even mentioned it to him, but pretence had never touched him. He was not the kind who could be tutored.

It was well past 4 p.m. Without talking much, they both decided to go for a Lake Geneva evening cruise tour. As they reached the ticket booth, Mansa, still feeling lost and grim, heard Abhijit ask the clerk, 'How much for two tickets?'

'Seventy-five Euros per person,' the clerk replied.

Abhijit smiled. 'Oh, that's quite an amount!'

The booking clerk said with a grin, 'Okay, sir, you pay for one and we can ferry your beautiful companion for free.'

Mansa could not even smile. Today, nothing in the world could have made her smile. She experienced a sort of foreboding. Something she couldn't decipher was tightening its hold over her.

The two-hour cruise included dinner and as soon as lights were turned on the ship, Abhijit made straight for the deck, holding her hand.

The snow-capped verdant peaks surrounding the lake, the azure water and sky, a faraway chapel and birds on the horizon made a perfect Lake Geneva painting, but Mansa couldn't care less. The superlative beauty of the lake failed to enchant her. She stood holding Abhijit's hand without uttering a word, completely oblivious to the celebrated beauty of the lake.

It was after 10 p.m. when they entered their room. As the room was a non-smoking one, after a change of clothes, Abhijit headed out for a smoke and Mansa quickly logged in to see if Rajan had sent his long, loving messages and poetry. Even if he did not mean any of it, she foolishly wanted to hear from him. They did not seem untrue to her, yet he had been so harsh to her.

As she heard Abhijit come in, she shut the laptop, pretending to be fast asleep. But sleep did not come to her. She stared at the false ceiling for most of the night without stirring even once, a deep sadness replacing her earlier enthusiasm.

In a few days' time she had seen it all—a plethora of emotions. Her tryst with this unseen man had led her to the heights of happiness and now to the depths of despair. Morning did not come quickly either. As Mansa opened her eyes, she saw Abhijit patiently waiting for her to wake up as he sat on a chair across their bed, admiring the beauty of the Swiss Alps and going through a newspaper. She saw him lift his gaze from the newspaper as he heard the rustle of sheets when Mansa turned on her side. He instantly got up to get them some tea.

Mansa casually looked around at the pastel blue furnishings in the room. The interior of the room was simple and tasteful. The modern wooden fixtures were elegant and practical, suitable to the needs of the contemporary traveller. In her euphoric state she had paid little attention to the finer details of the room. A person to whom décor mattered so much had failed to notice it—this was a shocker even to her.

Even though she was mostly in a frozen emotional state, whenever she thought of Rajan, it hurt. There was no respite from the mental torture. She consoled herself, trying to convince herself that since she would be in Geneva for many more days, there was no way that he would not come to meet her.

'Tea for you, Madam,' Abhijit's high-pitched, loving voice brought her back to the present. He asked, 'Should we order something in the room? The breakfast buffet time is over and I'm quite famished.'

Mansa nodded and leapt into the bathroom. As she brushed her teeth, her mind kept going over her conversation of the previous day with Rajan.

Abhijit called out to her again and the clutter of breakfast being served in the room made her realize that she had stayed for an unusually long time in the bathroom. She quickly went back to the room and in an effort to control her shaky thoughts, she decided to concentrate on enjoying her vacation with Abhijit and discard Rajan from her mind. She called up the reception for brochures and even made calls to the concierge to confirm the sightseeing plans for the day. Abhijit watched her, slightly amused, as it was the first time on the trip that he had seen any participation from her.

Mansa decided that she would not do any more injustice to Abhijit. He had shelled out a lot of his savings to provide her this vacation of her choice by extending the stay much beyond his official mandate to be with her and Malvika over the weekend.

They left for Mount Titlis and she fought hard not to allow Rajan's behaviour to destroy their trip. However, her mind kept going around the same circles. Although there was no denying the splendour and beauty of Titlis, her senses had been rendered incapable of enjoying anything. A deep gloom seized her. She was not sure when she would talk to Rajan next and what she would say to him. Friday was fast disappearing. A call had to be taken now.

The next morning, they were supposed to leave for London so that they could spend the weekend with Malvika, as she was returning from the cruise. Abhijit was to leave for New Delhi for a week on Monday afternoon, while Mansa was to remain in London with Malvika. Mansa was grateful that Abhijit had to go to New Delhi on Monday. She thought that his absence would lessen her guilt and she would worry less about Shonali because her dad would be with her.

Abhijit was to return to London later for a week again, and they were going to spend the last few days of their in London together. It was decided that Mansa would return to India thereafter and Abhijit would attend his conference in London before coming back to India finally, a week after Mansa. The programme was well-thought-out and meticulous. However, Mansa was restless. This two-day window looked great, as all three of them would be together. But she realized that if she went ahead to London, she would be further away from Rajan and whatever little chance she stood of seeing him would be gone. She had to do something about it now.

She decided to try to see if she could stay there a day or two longer. She felt like a trickster and schemer again, but she kept reminding herself 'everything is fair in love and war'. *And is this not the first time that you have felt such a strong emotion? So you have to somehow pull it off,* she thought. Her lovelorn mind went to the extent of thinking of faking an illness. She had heard and read the phrase 'crimes of passion' many times in stories, movies and newspapers, but had been bewildered by what it meant. Today, she was no longer judgmental, constantly praying to God to forgive her. To her, passion had seemed a very animal-like emotion and unbecoming of an evolved human being, but today she felt it was a divine force.

She knew for a fact that she would not have to stretch herself too much to get Abhijit to agree with what she wanted. She had never seen a more magnanimous individual than him. As they descended Mount Titlis, she held Abhijit's hand tightly, gave him a warm smile and said, 'This place is so beautiful! Such fresh and fragrant air. I could live here forever.'

Abhijit nodded and said, 'It's becoming increasingly difficult to find such fresh air in India even on the mountains, because of the indiscriminate felling of trees. How ruthlessly we are being deprived of our forest cover by crooked politicians, bureaucrats, the forest mafia and poachers.'

Mansa breathed a sigh of relief. Her plan had worked. She knew from here she could easily talk him into staying there for another night or two. She found herself asking, 'Abhi, don't you like these mountains and this solitude here with me? Let's spend the weekend here.'

Abhijit looked a bit befuddled, but couldn't say no to her while she was holding his hand. Once back to their room, Abhijit soon flopped on the bed out of exhaustion. Mansa knew she would have to wait till she was sure that he was fast asleep. She wasn't even sure if she would find Rajan online or would have to content herself by leaving him a message. She had a very brief wait. She stood near the window and gazed out at the street lined with eateries, watch and jewellery shops, which now had their shutters down and neon boards on, making a sharp contrast to the tall dark mountains behind. Barring a restaurant or two, the street looked deserted. Abhijit seemed to have fallen asleep as soon as he had hit the bed. She herself was nowhere near sleepy. She stood near the window motionless, to let Abhijit fall deeper asleep.

Quietly, she tiptoed with a mug of green tea in one hand and a pillow in the other towards the seating area in the porch and settled herself on a reclining chair there. Her laptop was already on the couch there. She sat comfortably on the chair and placed the laptop on her thighs. She stretched out her feet on the couch and faced the room, where she could see Abhijit. With great trepidation she went online. Not only was Rajan there, but many of his unread messages were there too, as she hadn't had a chance to log in the entire day. Strangely, he wanted to know which places she had visited and if he could help with more suggestions. He had even offered to have a bottle of wine delivered to her suite.

She read his message in horror, hurt again: *What's your room number? I want to send a bottle of wine to you both.*

She struggled to understand, *wine for me and Abhijit? From him? Do I say he is an old college acquaintance? Or does he think wine will make up for emotionally wounding me? Or is it a goodwill gesture?* What he was trying to say or do was beyond her comprehension.

She was slowly trying to collect her nerves to explore his mind and find out if he had meant whatever he had said yesterday or if he had been trying to gauge her reaction. Despite all the hurtful things he had said, he seemed very gentle and affable again. She again wondered to herself if all his display of love was fake.

She finally mustered the courage to ask him again: *Rajan, couldn't you drive by this side on Saturday or Sunday morning. Maybe I could see you from a distance, from my hotel window?*

Unexpectedly, she again unleashed a very harsh reaction from him.

Rajan: *Are we in high school? I'm in the suburbs of Geneva. Am I supposed to drive all the way—31 miles—to show myself to you?*

Mansa: *I feel inquisitive. You have never even posted a picture of yourself.*

Rajan: *It's too far. How will I find you in that Karol Bagh like place?*

Mansa: *Don't ask me how in this age of cars and mobile networks you would find a person. Where there is will, there is a way.*

Rajan: *I told you, I might be away on that day with some urgent office work.*

Mansa: *You did! So now I have two extra days, Saturday and Sunday. And I am sure at least you're free on Sunday?*

Rajan: *What will I tell my family? Why am I going to Geneva Business District? What will my mother-in-law think? She is travelling with us. Also I have to take my son to see a gymnastics show. Impossible. It's a hell of a busy day.*

Crestfallen and feeling deeply betrayed and embarrassed, Mansa didn't know what to say. She had once enjoyed ecstasy and happiness thinking of him and listening to say, a Sufi *qawwali* sent by him. And today all that was left of the relationship was pain and only throbbing pain. She felt like dying. She hurriedly signed out. Strangely, some part of her mind still said, *it's a joke. He wants to catch me off guard and will give me a big surprise*, while another part of her mind said, *It's all over. Why am I still hoping against all hope?*

With great difficulty she made it to her bed beside Abhijit, her heart heavy with grief. She knew a long, unending stretch of sleepless nights awaited her. She also knew that whatever he might have to say or do, mentally and emotionally he would never be able to bridge those 31 miles with her.

12

The Exit of Reverie

'Noise is a cruel ruler Who is always imposing Curfews.
While Stillness and quiet Break open the vintage Bottles,
Awake the real Band.'

—Hafiz

WHAT IS LOVE? Why are some people unable to express it, while others express it so loosely, devoid of any meaning? Why is love as hurtful as it is pleasurable? Why do people who love each other quarrel so much? Why does it lead to a state of either zero expectations or expectations of the highest order? Why is love the most abused, overused, misused and confused emotion of all times?

Various thoughts related to love crossed Mansa's mind. In her six-month-old online relationship with Rajan, they had fought several times; each time not talking for a couple of days and once almost for a month, making it a rocky, tempestuous and extremely volatile relationship. She tried building the answers based on her upbringing and as Abhijit had taught her. 'Attachments build expectations, expectations bring frustrations. One should always be motivated by nishkam (unattached) karma,' he would say.

The answer stared her in the face—expectations. She had landed on European soil with great expectations of seeing the man who had stirred and shaken her emotions like she had never experienced before. Mansa felt extremely guilty and hollow thinking about what had happened. She felt shame. She couldn't understand how a man so full of love and emotion could behave in such a harsh, rude manner. Her thinking was failing but at no time did she want to believe that he had no feelings for her and had just been having fun at her cost.

In addition to this trauma, she not only had to pull herself together, but also had to put on a brave face. After all, she had been instrumental in having their plans changed, for what she knew now was a mirage.

When she finally woke up the next morning feeling dead inside, even Abhijit noticed her lacklustre appearance. Attributing it to tiredness, broken sleep and the change in temperature, she did her best to look cheerful and went about the day as best as she could. Despite her efforts, wherever they went out—to scenic places, shopping arcades, restaurants, museums and cruises—her eyes looked out only for Rajan. She had a very strong feeling many times that he would suddenly appear from nowhere to have a hearty laugh at her state. Only by Sunday night was she reconciled to the fact that it hadn't been a joke and she was a fool of the first order for pinning her hopes like a high school girl on an utter stranger. That night, she did not feel like going online.

She had no answers to why such craziness had clouded her judgement. Whatever it was—attachment, attraction, infatuation, love—was it true or false? There were no right or wrong answers, but what she had got in return was extreme agony and she did not know when and how it was going to heal and how she was going to cope with her daily life under this pall of gloom.

Strangely enough, she did not even once hate Rajan. Although sometimes she did question why he had very cleverly planted seeds of love in her mind and what he expected from her. Clearly, he had never expected such a strange coincidence of being present in Switzerland at the same time as her and so soon. Maybe, being in such close proximity to one another had not been a part of his scheme of things and when it did happen, he chickened out.

Now it seemed that he was only looking for some online fun with her while she had become serious about their relationship, but still her heart was not ready to buy this. She was trying to justify his motives. She unsuccessfully tried to convince herself that only something very catastrophic would have caused him to not make the effort to meet her. She was even trying to believe that it was honesty on his part to not meet her, as it would never have been right for their families even if he did truly love her.

On Monday morning, on their entire train journey back to London she couldn't utter a single word to Abhijit. They went straight to Heathrow. Malvika joined them at the airport to see off Abhijit, who was to fly to India. Malvika was slightly cross that they had arrived on Monday instead of Friday, but when she saw her mother in such low spirits, she did not express her disappointment.

Unlike her overemotional mother, she was more of her Papa's girl, a sensible daughter of a sensible father, and had acquired his physical and mental traits. She was an exceptionally gifted, intelligent girl. Of medium height, slim, with a thick black mane and jet black eyes she looked very attractive. Added to that was her flawless sense of style, which she had inherited from her mother.

Mansa and Malvika went in a cab to Malvika's apartment near the college campus. She shared it with two other girls, an American and an Italian, both of whom were travelling at the moment, leaving the apartment completely to the mother-daughter.

The excitement of spending time with her daughter and sharing her apartment for the first time only momentarily distracted Mansa from thoughts of Rajan. As the car sped towards the campus, the urge to reconnect with him began mounting, as she had not gone online for two days now. She knew he had dealt her a blow, which would take time to heal.

Malvika was very excited to have her mother with her. She held on to her hand all the way home. Her apartment was located in a very green avenue, the entire expanse looking as though it had been bathed clean. Mansa in her mental turmoil was neither able to share her daughter's excitement nor was she able to admire the surroundings of Malvika's London abode. Malvika's apartment looked lively and inviting. Two of the bedrooms on the ground floor, which shared a common bathroom, were locked, as their occupants were away. The downstairs area also had a common drawing–dining area, which looked comfortably spacious to house three. A black, grey and white tapestry synchronized with the rest of the colour scheme of the apartment. The kitchen looked clean and comfortable too. It was an open kitchen attached to the drawing room on one side and had a small opening, a porch, overlooking the main road and other apartments across the road on the other. The porch held a broad comfortable chair and two easy stools. The entire set-up was practical and comfortable.

Malvika's room was upstairs, which she liked because of the attached bathroom and privacy. Malvika loved sitting on the steps while working on her laptop, submitting assignments and taking phone calls.

When Mansa entered the kitchen, as usual, she inspected it minutely and began her sprucing up mission. She needed a labour-intensive chore to come out of her current mood and to forget her mental angst. She wanted to completely drown herself in intensive physical activity. After three continuous hours of hard-core cleaning, the apartment and kitchen looked even livelier. While she was cleaning, simultaneously she also cooked a light meal of dal-rice with matar paneer. Malvika opened the gifts that Mansa had carried for her from India, exclaiming in delight at each of them. While Mansa cleaned and cooked, Malvika hung the latest framed family pictures, which Mansa had carried from India, in her room. Next, she stormed into the kitchen and wrapped Mansa in her arms from behind.

'Mom, it's not fair. You have just come. How much more do you want to slog? And thanks for the green top; it's exactly the shade I wanted.'

Overwhelmed by the warmth of her daughter's hug, Mansa couldn't control her sobs. Some of it was due to the pain caused by Rajan's incredible rudeness and some in gratitude for the comfort of warmth from her daughter, which she so badly needed.

Malvika was startled, but said gently, 'Mom, now you better come and sit with me. Are you missing Shona? Enough of all this. Please wash up. I'll make you some green tea.'

Mansa pulled Malvika to her and gave her a warm hug and a kiss on her cheek—the scolding mixed with pampering she got from her daughter touched Mansa's heart. She went up to Malvika's room to freshen up. The sight of her laptop on her bed, tempted her again, but as Malvika was around, she decided to check for any fresh message from Rajan later. She still found it hard to reconcile with the idea that he had been within a small radius from her and had made no effort to meet her.

She came down quickly to the porch after a hurried wash. Malvika was waiting for her with tea, cookies and some namkeens, which Mansa had brought for her from India. Some tales from Mansa's childhood and some from Malvika's childhood resonated in the apartment, with mother and daughter catching up with each other about every small detail of their lives. Mansa's participation remained dull and insignificant, unable to lessen the heaviness in her heart.

Malvika had some assignments to do for submission late

that evening and Mansa thought that would be the most appropriate time to see what Rajan had to say about what had happened. She was in too much pain to think straight. Post-dinner, they both lounged around, sitting with their laptops. Malvika was sitting on the steps, while Mansa chose to sit in the porch to get an outside view as well as to draw some warmth from the kitchen, although the apartment was very cosy. As she logged in, she saw a few of his messages, which had accumulated over the last two days. Mostly they asked why she had been upset or if she was angry. It all seemed like small talk compared to the magnitude of pain she had been going through.

Was it possible that a person, who had ceaselessly claimed to love her so much and had displayed such intense emotions for her for almost six months, had never meant any of it? She had no answer to that question. In fact, she had many questions and no answers.

She was not in a mental frame to reply to his subtle queries. She just browsed for a while and feeling dejected and disinterested, logged out without answering. Instead, she decided to go out for a walk, but in her sadness, she felt too fatigued and lacked the energy to continue for long. She returned home soon.

As she came in, Malvika's cheerful voice greeted her, 'Mom, I've submitted my assignment. Let's watch a movie. I have bought your favourite coffee ice cream for you. Let's get it out.'

She tried her best to feel involved and share her daughter's enthusiasm, but failed to be her usual self. Time and again, she felt distracted from the plot of the movie they were watching and was lost in analysing what she had just gone through. She knew she was not being able to reciprocate her daughter's kind gestures. Tiredness due to her long journey coupled with emotional fatigue caused her to fall asleep while the movie was still going on.

She did not feel much better when she woke up the next morning. But she thanked God that without help and maids, doing housework for the next fortnight would at least keep her physically occupied, so she could think less about Rajan and what he had done to her. The view outside the glass windowpane looked cold and hazy. It had rained and snowed continuously for the second day today. She had no intention of leaving the apartment for any reason.

She devoted the entire day to cleaning and reorganizing her daughter's room. She knew that if she rested, she would drift into a deep depression. Every now and then, tears rolled down her cheeks at the disappointment of not being able to see Rajan. She tried hard to keep her dignity by not crying when her daughter was around, as there were no reasons in her life—as Malvika knew it—that she could attribute her tears to if her daughter asked. She fought very hard to keep her spirits up.

By the sixth day, she still had not managed to drag herself out of her despondency and so far she had not been able to strike a normal conversation with Rajan. They had had a few short exchanges in which she had expressed her displeasure at what had happened and he had said that he had had genuine preoccupations. He had even threatened that if she did not believe him they had no reason to continue the relationship and he would delete her. Although prudence and righteousness demanded that she stay away from him and even delete him after what had happened, her heart was not in her control. She actually believed in her true selfless love for him.

That day, her weakness for him was getting the better of her again and her stance against him was mellowing. Her fatal attraction to him was getting ready to forgive this perfidious episode. She was miserably failing in her resolve to keep away from him. Terrified and anxious, she opened her account in a somewhat reconciliatory mood. She did not find Rajan online. She felt a bit disappointed. Lest she change her mind, she decided to linger on his profile for some time to wait for him, but she could not access it. She couldn't understand what was happening. A while later she realized that she had been blocked from seeing his profile.

She shut down and kept the laptop away in disbelief. This was the last thing she could have ever expected from him. As if what had already been meted out to her was not enough, this felt like the final nail in the coffin of their relationship. She felt a migraine attack besieging her. She sank on the couch and felt as if she would pass out. She had no idea of the date, day, time or place. Was it a brief moment or had ages passed? For her, time stood still and so did everything around her. Something within her died that minute. She went through the same feeling of personal loss and gloom she had experienced when her parents had died. Her faith in humanity and men in general stood shattered.

Mansa had no idea when she had logged in or out and for how much time she lay in that state. When she opened her eyes, it was late evening. She was still on the couch and Malvika was bent over her, asking anxiously, 'Mom, Mom! What happened? What's wrong? Are you okay? Your cheeks feel damp and eyes look swollen. I was at college for almost six to seven hours. And you hadn't even latched the door from inside. Did you bathe? Have you eaten? You look so unwell! Is it a migraine? What's the matter? Should I call Papa?'

Mansa barely managed to say, 'Migraine', which was not true, but she had to say something.

Malvika went on, 'Mom, ever since I was a child, you got migraines only on Mahashivratri. Isn't it unusual that you are getting it here in London and that too at this time of the year?'

Mansa said irritably, 'Malu, is it a rule that I can only get it then and never before or after? Not all ailments follow a periodic cycle.'

'Oh Mom!' Amused, Malvika said, 'You forget you are talking to a doctor in the making. I know all that, but you and Papa are some freak cases worth studying and researching. I have never heard of any parents, who both suffer from such unusual syndromes. But Shonali and I are very lucky and proud to have you both as parents.'

The question of whether Abhijit and Mansa were betrothed in their small endogamous Brahmin community due to their unique illnesses, when no one else would willingly take them again, crossed Mansa's mind.

She did not feel like reacting to Malvika. Her system was undergoing cataclysms. All she wanted was to be left alone. No sound, no light, no movement, nothing! She was failing to hide her emotional upheaval and was forced to plead that

Malvika should leave her alone.

Malvika did not quite understand her mother's devastated state. She had always seen her mother as a youthful, vivacious bundle of energy. People called her an 'ageless diva', and Malvika had always been proud of her mother's perfect looks. Today she appeared old, with dark circles under her eyes and appeared very tired, something Malvika had never seen before.

Malvika decided to let her be for the time being. She herself was extremely tired and hungry. She went towards the refrigerator in search of something to eat and decided to request her mom to at least have a bite for her sake. But seeing her condition, she finally decided to not disturb her, as she appeared to be sleeping again. With a thepla roll in one hand, she climbed the steps quickly and quietly so as not to wake up her mother lying down on the couch. Once on her bed, tired after a long day's slogging, she also fell asleep.

Waking up two hours later, Malvika found her mom still on the couch, which worried her. Ever since her mother had entered her apartment, despite her protests, she had been on one agenda or the other, from cooking and cleaning to making her as comfortable as possible. While she attended college, her mother dedicated the day to either cleaning up or resetting her room, shelves and cupboards, or making snacks and elaborate menus for them. In the evening, they went for short walks in the surrounding parks or went shopping or had dinner in some restaurant close by. But Malvika had noticed that her mother was not laughing these days.

Deep in her thoughts, Malvika went to the kitchen and saw that there had been no activity in it. Over the past few days, her mother had already cooked many *dals*, gravies and vegetables and packed and stored them for her daughter, but on this day it looked as if she had not even stepped into the kitchen. She wondered what could have happened today. It seemed like her mother had never left the couch since morning.

Malvika wanted to make some special effort for her mother, so she boiled some rice and rearranged a meal from her stock. She sat beside her mom, stroked her face gently and tried making small talk. Feeling grateful, and in a bid to shake herself out of her present state, Mansa made a great effort to sit up and put something in her mouth, but she had lost all desire to eat. She swallowed some water for the first time since the morning and made straight for the bathroom. She had no idea whether Malvika had eaten or not. She just wanted to resign herself to a state of thoughtlessness, but it could not be.

Once back on the couch, she was surrounded by the same thoughts. She wondered if being blocked by Rajan had actually happened to her or she had hallucinated and dreamt it. She wasn't sure if she was still alive. She toyed with the idea of emailing Rajan to tell him how grossly unfair he had been to her, but changed her mind. She had no idea why a woman like her, who had always been so sought after in all the circles she had moved in, but never felt attracted to anyone before, now cared so much for an unseen person.

She felt ashamed of wanting to email him after being treated so badly. For some unknown reason, her desperation overtook her and she actually wanted him to understand how unreasonable he had been . At the same time, she wondered if a person who had cast her aside like a dead fly was capable of understanding what he had done to her. And what use would it ever be if he did? She would never be able to get over what had happened.

The ties forged online seemed so real to some people, including herself, mused Mansa whereas they were nothing more than a joke or a pastime to others. The emotions and pain they were capable of generating were so tangible, so real. Mansa felt as though she had been a victim of someone's cruel joke.

How much he had followed her for months, trying to convince her of his yearning and love. Couldn't he have had the patience to wait a few days for her to restore her mood? Her few days of silence had invoked such a harsh response from him. What was her fault? That she had expressed a desire to see him? And when it did not happen, she had expressed some anger over not meeting him? Did she have no right to do that? Are such expressions not supposed to be a part of online relationships? Are there unsaid norms in such relationships? She had no explanation to justify what he had done and why he had done it, even then, she had a strong urge to reconnect and not lose touch entirely, probably because he was her first and maybe last love. She felt a strong desire, which she could not understand, to reconcile with him. So, she finally convinced herself that deleting and blocking her was not entirely his fault. He had tried a lot to talk to her, waited for six days for her to answer and sent several messages, but she had remained adamant by ignoring what he was trying to say.

Who has ever won a battle against themselves?

Finally, when sleep seemed miles away and her heart and mind knew no respite, her emotions out of her control, she wrote him an email. She was in a terribly broken mental state, had lost all sense of time and had no idea if it was day or night. But she was sure that by now he would have reached LA from his Europe vacation. She poured out her heart in her email:

Rajan,
I was about to reconcile with you but couldn't you wait a little longer? I never meant to write and don't know why I am doing so. I don't want to talk to you as I am very angry and hurt but let's just stay connected as you said that permanent detachment was not possible.
Mansa

A day passed by and there was no response. Very worked up and exhausted from her emotional turmoil, she decided to write another email.

Rajan,
You deleted me when I was the one who was wronged and should have deleted you. Right before leaving India I asked you, did you really mean it when you said you were asking for me in your prayers and you said you never say things that you don't mean.
And you did not even want to meet the person you were asking for in your prayers? Is that not strange?
Mansa

Hope is a strange gift of God to human beings. It helps them to survive and keep going. Maybe human beings invented punarjanam or reincarnation, Paleogenesis, Metempsychosis, and other such philosophies and concepts so that we could console ourselves that even when this body dies, we will still live on in some form.

Mansa's hope was quite akin to the philosophy of rebirth, which carries the hope of a new genesis. Even though the relationship had died in one form, maybe it could still be kept alive in another form. A flicker of hope was still alive despite the anguish she was going through. She thought that as soon as he read her email, he would understand and be apologetic—he would respond and immediately add her back. The most painfully long forty-eight hours, where she had waited every nanosecond for his response had passed, but she heard nothing from him. Had it not been for him not meeting her, then deleting and blocking her, she would probably have inundated him with messages by now.

She had realized early in their relationship that Rajan had a fragile ego and used retributive language; if their relationship had any chances of surviving, she would have to be patient and abandon her ego to him. This time, things were very different, but she had still made all conciliatory efforts and the ball was in his court now. Today was the third day she hadn't eaten anything despite Malvika's best efforts. Mansa was thankful to God that Malvika was so absorbed in her exams, labs and assignments that beyond the first day, she could not understand much about what her mother was going through. She usually left by 8 a.m. and came back only after 5 p.m., when she barely had enough energy to have a short exchange with her mother. Hence, she had no idea about the turmoil that Mansa was going through.

Finally, in the late evening Mansa got a message from Rajan.

A hopeful enthusiasm triggered some energy in her.

Rajan had written:

What crap, we have already been over it again and again. I said I was genuinely busy.

She was dumbfounded. She had not expected him to be completely unapologetic and indifferent. There was no effort to understand, empathize or even add her back. Reading his terse reply, Mansa lost all self-control and started weeping uncontrollably. Scared lest her daughter see her in this condition in the middle of the night, she decided to take a firm decision on this one-way relationship. She wrote again:

> *Rajan,*
> *Are words not the same as they mean? Do they have a different meaning for different people? How many times did you say you loved me, were crazy about me, and could not do without me? Did I say all that even once? I even asked you how many women you have been this close to before. You said three, as you are married and had been married once before. All the poetry, songs, sweet nothings, what was all that? Did they not mean anything?*
> *Mansa*

Feeling foolish, knowing it was futile, without even waiting for his response, she wrote again:

> *Rajan,*
> *Please ignore my previous mail. It was quite unnecessary.*
> *Mansa*

Again there was no response for one full day. And finally

the next night, another mail appeared:

We are done and I have said that before. What is the need for mailing this kind of crap?

Mansa read the text incredulously. Bruised and battered to the core, feeling very vulnerable and immersed in self-pity, without even caring for her self-esteem, she wrote again:

Rajan,
Please don't do this to me. I haven't been able to sleep or eat for the fourth day today. Please don't send me back with a permanent bad taste of London in my mouth and such bitter memories.
Even I don't want to talk to you but please just let's stay connected or from now on I am going to dread the month of November forever. It's even my birthday month. It's really not much to ask.
Mansa

After writing this and feeling some comfort in believing that she had done her best, she was able to get some sleep. She had been down in the hall on the couch for a fourth consecutive day now. She had no strength even to climb up to Malvika's room.

Next morning, when Malvika climbed down, she saw her mother awake. Mansa told her that she wanted to clean up and eat something. She did not herself understand where this resolve came from. The pain still remained, but her mechanical movements seemed improved. She quietly ate a paratha Malvika had heated for her.

She knew mentally where she was heading. The decision she had made gave her some strength. She knew forgetting Rajan was not going to be possible, but as her love for him was deep, pure and undying, she realized that to reduce the pain, she would have to make a sincere effort to forgive him and forget the episode.

She decided that at night she would make one final attempt to rationalize with him and then face the outcome. The day passed with an unusually low momentum. She felt a little more in control of herself. She spent the day chanting and praying and by night felt less deluded, as she wrote:

> *Love for you may be a meaningless joke. I have no right to express the desire to meet you. I have no right to express anger at not being able to meet you. I get deleted when I display any anger at not being able to meet you. Did you want a relationship with a robot or someone made of flesh and blood?*

Unexpectedly, like a clap of thunder, she had a reply back from him:

> *What crap do you write time and again? Never write back after this.*
> *Rajan Chopra*

A decision by then had already been made in Mansa's mind and she wrote her final letter to him.

> *Time and again whatever I write, you have called it crap. You have categorically asked me to not write back to you. It will be unethical for me to ever write to you*

again. Maybe I will see a therapist or go soul-healing and get over all this.

Goodbye and take care of yourself as this is my last mail to you.

Mansa

Not only had her heart been badly broken, but her spirit felt crushed too.

Time passed at a dead pace. Just two days were left for Abhijit to join them in London. He was scheduled to stay in a hotel, as he was on an official trip. Just one day of Malvika's semester exams was left. In a day's time her apartment mates were going to return too. It had been decided that Malvika and Mansa would join Abhijit in his Central London hotel and invite Madhulika's family over for dinner before Mansa left for India. Thereafter, Abhijit was going to stay till his official business was over, and Malvika would also stay with her father in the hotel till she had her college break.

Mansa had been repeatedly asking herself over the last two days of her London stay that had she stayed in a better hotel in Geneva, he would have come to see her, as he had the audacity to call the place where she was staying Sheraton. Or had this also been inane talk, like all his love tales had been?

Two days later, she boarded her flight to India. On her way back, she thought that although this was the most fathomless and piercing pain she had ever experienced. *What use is a life if you had never loved, never had your heart broken, and never felt the pain, never felt alive? You might as well never live!* She did not regret loving him and knew she could not stop doing so.

Part II

13

Kaal Chakra

'Never was there a time when I did not exist, nor you, nor all
these kings; nor in the future shall any of us cease to be. As the
embodied soul continuously passes, in this body, from childhood
to youth to old age, the soul similarly passes into another body
at death. A sober person is not bewildered by such a change.'
—Srimad Bhagwad Gita

THE GOLF TRACKS were engulfed with the warmth of the
golden sunshine, invigorating and energizing the atmosphere.
Oblivious to her surroundings, Mansa plodded tentatively
along the path tightly gripping Shonali's hand and reflecting
upon her recent emotional injury. She constantly mused she had
never even hurt an ant so what did she do to deserve this pain?

The bright and sunny morning greeted the last day of the
last month of the year, bidding adieu to the eventful year of
Mansa's life. The days were still short and a slightly unpleasant

chill hit her spine, further shrinking her narrow frame. Here, there and elsewhere, winter foliage was withering, making the gloom in Mansa's heart heavier and harder to bear.

Usually, these had been her favourite months. Mansa had always found the greenery surrounding the golf course strewn with autumn leaves very romantic. She could endlessly gaze and marvel at the beauty of a barren tree. She found the colour, texture and shapes fascinating, a divine gift. Even while reading, every now and then she would lift her gaze from the book to rest on the graceful arch of a branch. Sometimes, even while sipping tea in her front portico, reclined on a rocking chair, her restless gaze always found solace in a tree, flowers or a bird perched in the garden. But at the moment, she walked unmindful of everything around her, including herself.

The pain was very recent and so overwhelming that she constantly wondered if she would ever feel interested in anything again. Oddly enough, she did not even wish to come out of it, as she felt bizarrely connected to the person who had caused this pain. Sometimes, she felt as though her heart was being ripped apart into pieces. At other times, she felt as if it was being squeezed tightly.

Now, here she was—every now and then on the verge of tears. Intermittently, during the last few days, she had sobbed loudly when no one was within earshot. Nothing held her interest; even shopping, which was one of her favourite mood lifters, did not interest her. She was not sure if she would ever feel like looking beautiful again. Her steps were heavy due to her overwhelming grief and she barely managed to stagger along.

It had been a week since she had returned from Europe.

And this was the first time that she had stepped out of the house, after Bela, and Shonali had coaxed her to go out, as Abhijit was coming back that night and would be devastated to see her in this state. Mansa, contemplating how pained Abhijit would be to see her so depressed, had tried her utmost best to get back to her normal routine by stepping out in the morning, if not for a jog or to go to the gym, then at least to make an effort to walk, which she hadn't done since she had returned.

Leaving her bed after six days, she felt as if she had almost forgotten how to walk. Lack of food and sleep had dulled her spirits further. Unable to walk further, she decided to do something she had never done before. She sat down on a bench near the pond, where she usually saw older people sitting, while she herself used to briskly sway past them. Her mind wandered to what she still thought of as the sweetest and the bitterest memories of her life.

A sudden bark from a stray dog undid Mansa's trance. She realized she had been sitting on the bench for over an hour now with her eyes shut. She did not find Shonali around. She looked at her phone and saw a message from her daughter: *Mom, you rest. I'll jog for however long you want to sit around the tracks.*

Almost at the same time, far away from behind a clump of trees she saw a figure in a bright sports T-shirt emerging. As it came closer, she smiled slightly, as she could see what a stunner and head-turner her younger daughter appeared even from a distance. While Malvika, her older daughter, had inherited her father's looks, Shonali was entirely Mansa's replica.

Shonali's happiness knew no bounds when she saw her

mother smile. She stretched her hands to help her mother to stand up and with Mansa leaning on Shonali, they walked together hand in hand towards their home. As they entered the apartment, it was almost that time of the day when she used to chat on and off with Rajan. She felt so weak and exhausted that she immediately crashed onto her bed. The next thing she remembered was being shaken awake at around 3 p.m.

Mansa felt much calmer upon waking up and thanked her daughter and maid for being so considerate and encouraging during her days of illness. She even agreed to have some kadhi khichdi to muster some strength to bathe, which she hadn't cared to do in so many days. The only reason that Mansa had forced herself to be up today was Abhijit's impending arrival from London. She knew that seeing her in this state would have upset him greatly and he would want to know what the reason was. She thanked God that Abhijit's flight was landing in the evening, which might lead him to pay less attention to her condition, although Shonali had been continuously updating Abhijit about her mother's health.

As Abhijit entered the house, he straightaway came to the bedroom. When he entered the room, she was sitting up in bed with her back resting on a pillow, futilely trying to concentrate on some television programme. She hadn't even thought about her work or office once since she had come home.

Abhijit first frowned at her appearance and then wrapped her in his arms. He felt shocked when he held her. She appeared more shrunken and much lighter than when he had seen her less than a week ago. He didn't say much. He kept looking at her intently and then lighting a cigarette, left the room to go out in the open. He wondered what might have happened to Mansa, but found no answers. She didn't seem to have any fever. His mind raced, thinking of which specialist to take her to first thing in the morning.

Despite Mansa's protests that she was okay and didn't need to see a doctor, Abhijit took her to their family physician, who happened to be a close family friend too and was Abhijit's bachelorhood buddy. The doctor suggested some detailed check-up. Abhijit felt awfully upset and even blamed himself for not having looked after her well enough during his hectic travelling. Abhijit's concern for her further compounded Mansa's grief, sickness and guilt, which still haunted her.

He tried his level best to make conversation with her many a times, but seeing her lack of interest, he felt resigned. He had no choice, but to wait for the reports. On their way back home from the clinic, she rested her head on his shoulders and he kept stroking her hair. Mansa's eyes welled up every now and then. She just couldn't get Rajan off her mind even in Abhijit's presence. Her brutally broken relationship and the untold miseries in its wake remained in her heart. She could not even reveal anything about it to anyone and it was taking a very heavy toll on her emotional and psychological health.

She kept thinking about what Tushita had told her when she had fallen on the jogging tracks before going to Europe— that it was a karmic fall, but she had not taken it seriously. When Tushita had called her up to find out about her Europe trip and if she had enjoyed it, Mansa decided to ask her over, as Sapna was also coming to see her.

She again felt like asking Abhijit if they should try

alternate healing therapies for his recurrent nightmares and her migraines. She hadn't asked Abhijit about this in a long time due to the fear of his stubborn refusal. Too wary of proposing it herself, she heard herself say, 'Tushita and Sapna are coming over to see me. Will you also spend some time with us?'

Abhijit looked at her, pressed her hand and smiled as if she had demanded something impossible. He said good-naturedly, 'I will sit with you and your friends till you chuck me out.'

Mansa too couldn't help but smile. She was trying hard to be as normal as possible with Abhijit. Abhijit kept holding her hand tight till he helped her into bed. It was early evening and she was beginning to shiver despite the heating in the room. Securing her tightly under two thick layers of blankets, Abhijit left the room quietly. He was very anxious, as there appeared no apparent illness and yet, Mansa looked extremely depressed and seemed to be losing her sleep, appetite and vitality so rapidly that it was becoming a grave cause of concern for him.

When the bell rang, Bela ushered Sapna into the living room, Abhijit was the first to greet her. He was not sure whether to inform Sapna about how unwell Mansa looked or to ask Sapna if she had any inkling of what was happening to Mansa. He was still wondering what to say, when the bell rang again. He knew it would be Tushita. He looked up and saw a professor-like lady in her mid-thirties, slightly plump, with a charming smile being escorted in by Bela. He got up to welcome her and said, 'You must be Tushita.'

She smiled and nodded in affirmation. He was wondering whether to wake up Mansa or not. He was still wondering, when he saw a pale Mansa walk towards them with Bela at her side. Her appearance made him even more anxious. Sapna couldn't suppress her shock at the sight of Mansa's frailty. 'Oh my God! Look at you…what have you done to yourself?'

Tushita also said gently, 'Mrs Mansa Bhargav, you don't look the same. Where is your ever charming self?'

Mansa tried smiling, but instead let out a soft moan. She held on to Sapna's hand and greeted Tushita. All three sat close together. Abhijit decided to leave them alone for a while till tea was served. A couple of times, Mansa thought that maybe she should confess to her good friend Sapna, as that might make her feel lighter, but she could not say anything in the presence of her husband and Tushita. None of them knew where to begin for a brief while.

Sapna began by asking, 'How's Malvika doing in London? And did you meet your old chum Madhulika too?'

Mansa placidly replied, 'Yes. Madhu is fine. We hung out together quite a lot.'

She turned to Tushita and asked, 'Tushi dear, you often mention and praise your Guru Ma for her soul-healing abilities. Is it possible for me to meet her? In London, I saw an uncanny dream of being surrounded by water and have been feeling weird ever since. Maybe meeting her would help. I have never had such dreams before. And for all we know, Abhijit may also find some respite from his sleep-walking and recurrent childhood nightmares with the help of Guru Ma.'

Tushita, only too eager to help, said, 'Why not? Sure. You let me know when you would like to come.'

'I would like to come and meet her as soon as possible, but I am not sure if Abhijit would come at all. He lacks faith in alternate healing and such therapies,' Mansa replied.

Sensing Mansa's eagerness, Tushita immediately dialled the ashram's number to seek an appointment for Mansa. She was informed that she would get a call the following day to confirm her request for a personal darshan with Ma. Soon, they were joined by Abhijit for tea.

Abhijit asked curiously, 'What were you talking about? Who is seeking an appointment for whom and regarding what?'

Tushita, a volunteer at the ashram and a very spiritually inclined person, attempted to satiate Abhijit's curiosity. She tried expounding the ashram philosophy as taught by Guru Ma: 'There are three ways we can hurt or heal people—by thought, speech and action. During the course of our lives, we meet many people whom we may intentionally or unintentionally hurt by way of thought, speech or action. One has to constantly seek forgiveness from people whom one might have hurt during the present or any past lives. According to Guru Ma's philosophy of Kaal Chakra, which is also stated in the Srimad Bhagvad Gita, in our physical body, we all go through karmic cycles or perform various types of karmas, good and bad, knowingly or unknowingly.

'Since they cannot be acquitted or balanced in one single lifetime, the journey of the soul continues till nirvana is achieved, after accumulating karmas. As the soul evolves, the balance of good karmas goes on increasing and once the debts towards bad karmas have been paid, the soul or atman merges with the parmatma or almighty. The aim of every living soul is to increase the good balance so as to move towards the higher self faster for mukti or salvation.'

Abhijit, who was listening very intently, said, 'I am a very simple person with a very clear philosophy—do good karma in a detached manner without worrying too much about the fruits of your action.'

Mansa always found such discussions, as circular as they were, interesting and absorbed every word. She hopefully looked at Abhijit and asked, 'So I can go?'

'Where?' Abhijit asked.

'To the ashram to seek Guru Ma's blessings. Maybe I'm feeling so low and suffer from migraines because of some bad karma.' Uttering this, Mansa couldn't control a sob, further worrying Abhijit.

To everyone's surprise, he offered, 'I will take you myself, dear. Can't let you go by yourself in this state.'

His offer made her eyes even moister; struck by her own foolishness in reciprocating her husband's boundless, unselfish love for her by falling in love with a person she had never seen and was not likely to ever meet. These thoughts continuously magnified her pain. She wanted to be alone to cry to her heart's content.

Seeing her so unsettled and unwell, her friends got up. Tushita left with a promise to call her back the next day with an appointment. Just before Sapna left, Mansa quickly confided in her about what had happened in Europe. Sapna gripped her friend's hands and said, 'Look, you have done nothing wrong, absolutely nothing. So don't feel guilty. Come out of this. You did not go out looking for a guy to fall in love with. It just happened. So, stop blaming yourself. You also had no expectations from this relationship, over and above an emotional connect. Now that clearly also has not been reciprocated. Obviously, he does not deserve your emotions, so stop mourning over it. This unnecessary grief and guilt is not going to take you anywhere, so be strong and get yourself out of this mess.'

She even demanded Rajan's mail ID to give him a piece of her mind for misleading and pushing her innocent friend into such a hopeless situation, but Mansa refused to give it to her. In fact, in response to her counselling, Sapna only received a blank stare from Mansa.

14

The Invisible Lands

'The sun will stand as your best man and whistle
When you have found the courage to marry forgiveness
When you have found the courage to marry Love...'

—Hafiz

Next morning, Mansa received a call from the ashram Mansa had been given an appointment for the very next day and Abhijit confirmed that he would accompany her. Tushita rung-up to inform her that she would also go to make things easier for Mansa.

The next day, Tushita reached Mansa's place on time. As the car rode ahead, the road culminated in a circular path, with an imposing temple-like structure at its centre. The structure was completely white with thick heavy wooden doors adorned with mounted brass engravings. They parked the car in front of the structure alongside many other cars. As they alighted, they were immediately ushered inside by a volunteer. They were led inside deeper and deeper into the edifice. A white sari-clad volunteer and Tushita led them around a rectangular meditation hall. They stopped together in front of a wooden door similar to the main door, but smaller in size, although it could not have been less than 8 feet tall. The décor of the entire ashram was very clean and simple. The most impressive part was the stillness and complete silence. So far, they had not heard a single utterance, although the central meditation hall, which had natural sunlight filtering in through the roof, was full of people in deep meditation. Even the volunteer had not spoken a single word so far.

The volunteer turned back after dropping them and gestured to them to go inside. Tushita gently pushed the door open. As they entered, they saw a woman in her mid-sixties sitting on a milk-white mattress. Three white sheets were arranged around it. The walls of the room were completely barren, barring a light and a fan whirring from the ceiling. The woman sat cross-legged on the mattress and appeared to be meditating. The three of them carefully and quietly perched themselves on the sheets. Within minutes, Guru Ma opened her eyes. She had a rare air of peace and sobriety. Her radiance was unsurpassable. They couldn't recall seeing anyone with such an aura. She was wearing a white cotton sari just like any other disciple, but what distinguished her from the others were the unparalleled charm and the depth of understanding and affection in her eyes.

All three prostrated themselves at her feet to seek her blessings. Ma gently touched each one's forehead. Then she questioningly looked at Mansa, as though she had been waiting for her to come. Mansa's eyes welled up and Ma signalled to Tushita and Abhijit to leave the room. They both left the room and crossed the corridor to the main meditation hall, where they quietly settled down on the white sheets. Mansa couldn't stop sobbing at Maa's warm and reassuring touch. Ma too did not stop her from crying.

Finally, Mansa forced herself to utter, 'Help me, Ma. Show me the way. I am marooned in deep sorrow and I dread the times ahead. I think I will never be able to get over my experience.' Ma kept looking at her warmly, encouraging her to speak further.

Finally, Mansa managed to say, 'These days I'm always very troubled…Ma! I don't get any sleep, don't like anything and keep thinking about the man I befriended online. I also dread the next month.' She broke down again, unable to speak further.

Ma asked, 'Why do you dread next month?'

Mansa replied, 'Ma, I dread my migraine, which I suffer from every Mahashivratri—ever since my childhood.'

Ma asked, 'Is that all?'

'No, Ma, there is more. But I can't share it at the moment. Ma, please help me.' Mansa continued sobbing, clutching at Ma's hand.

Ma said gently, 'Then you have to trust me completely with your consciousness. Will you allow me to take you to your past life or lives to see how we can help you? Sometimes, when we don't find solutions or answers to our problems in the present life, we may find them in our past lives. We may sometimes have to alter or mend our karmic cycle to heal ourselves.'

Mansa, still clutching her hand, nodded in the affirmative with a little trepidation.

Ma continued, 'Have you ever had regression therapy before?'

'No, Ma.'

'Do you have a history of dreams?'

'No, Ma, although my husband does. He has seen the same nightmare over and over again since his childhood.'

'Would you like me to take you to your past life?'

'Yes, Ma.'

'If you see things you don't want to share with me, then you don't have to do so. Just raise or flicker your hand and I will stop, so that we can come back to the present.'

Mansa nodded and said, 'Ma, I have a question. I have heard that sometimes people are not able to come back to their present lives and as a result, turn insane. I am only scared of that. I don't want to dangle between two lives. As it is, I am very torn in my current state of affairs; I don't want to be torn between two lives.'

A deep smile of understanding adorned Ma's face and she said, 'We are all subjects to and subjects of karma. Whatever happens is probably predestined so if it is the fate of some people to remain in their past lives, so be it.

'What we can do at best from our end is to practise detached karma without the expectation of any reward. This is our karma bhumi, our karmic field. Whatever karma we perform today by virtue of thought, speech and action, the good and bad of that action will continue with us even when we have left this body for a new one. And unless we clear all our karmic debts, where the good deeds outweigh the bad ones, we cannot expect complete, blissful, eternal happiness and our soul will not find salvation or oneness with the supreme consciousness, which means that this cycle of birth and death, the Kaal Chakra, will continue. Just remember this—we have lived before and we will live many more lives.'

Although Mansa had been raised on this premise, today her grief did not allow her to absorb anything.

She softly said, 'Ma, I would like to share everything that I see with you. I completely trust you.' She prostrated herself before Ma.

Guru Ma directed her to lie down straight and asked her to empty her mind.

Guru Ma began,

'Just be blank and think of nothingness.
Your body seems light.
You are drifting into sleep.
A very deep, calm sleep.
You see a tunnel, a very long one.
You want to cross it and see what lies on the other side.
So you slowly start treading the tunnel.

While treading the tunnel, do look around everywhere and do stop wherever you feel like to see what holds your attention. And when you don't feel like going any further, just come back here. Do you see anything?'

Mansa did not answer.

Guru Ma repeated, 'Do you see anything?'

In a broken voice, Mansa spoke, 'Peepal tree... three

children... playing... terrace overhead... sun...' And then she screamed loud enough to penetrate the serenity of the ashram.

Abhijit and Tushita came running inside. Mansa struggled to wake up, her voice fading. She lost consciousness. Guru Ma gestured at Abhijit and Tushita to sit down quietly and calmly. Abhijit felt very agitated and restless seeing Mansa unconscious. He had half a mind to rush her to a doctor and had great difficulty in suppressing his anxiety. Sensing Abhijit's discomfiture, Ma touched his forehead to comfort him.

Guru Ma said, 'As it was not safe for her to go back any further into her past, we did not go all the way. It would not be a great idea to further stress her, as she is suffering from some emotional and psychological barriers. Such psychosomatic illnesses have to be treated very patiently. She may have to come for repeated sessions.'

Abhijit, who had no idea of Guru Ma's medical credentials, was amazed to hear medical vocabulary from her. He was later very surprised to find out from Tushita that Ma was very well-qualified, with degrees from top American medical schools like John Hopkins and Yale. He couldn't help but feel embarrassed, as he had underestimated her, thinking she could be a quack. Now he felt relieved as he always valued education over everything else and his respect for Guru Ma increased manifold.

Suddenly, all heads turned to Mansa, as she fluttered her eyelids and tried lifting herself up. She straightened her dupatta, as she sat upright.

Ma asked, 'How do you feel?'

Mansa actually felt lighter and calmer, as though she had wiped some mist off a pane of glass on a winter morning and some much-needed sunlight had filtered in. She softly conveyed that she felt better. Guru Ma nodded and gestured to them to leave. Tushita led them all out, as it was time for Ma to meditate.

They all prostrated in reverence and proceeded towards the gate from which they had entered. As they crossed the gate, Tushita assured Mansa that she would fix the next appointment for her with Guru Ma at the earliest possible date. They were just about to sit in their car, when they were handed over a slip by a volunteer. As the car roared, they read the slip and found instructions for the next session, which was scheduled for the day after at 2 p.m.

Although Mansa was sitting in a car full of people, mentally she was in a vacuum. She was dull and quiet. Images of a peepal tree and the injustice meted out to her by Rajan constantly flashed before her eyes. As the driver rode in silence, the three of them chatted to cheer up Mansa. The traffic had been lighter than usual and they covered the distance to the ashram sooner than expected. As the car glided ahead the serene surroundings around the ashram instantly brought tranquillity to their minds. Soon they entered the ashram and Mansa was lead into Guru Ma's room. The rest were directed to wait in the meditation hall.

Mansa prostrated before Ma and said, 'Ma, I have made up my mind to share everything with you; I want to reduce the hurt and pain caused by a very recent relationship.' She sobbed, holding Ma's hand.

Ma directed her to be calm. She didn't say anything, just caressed her hair gently and gestured her to lie down straight. Mansa stretched herself on the white sheet before Ma.

Ma said, 'I shall repeat the instructions like last time, and you move ahead from where you had stopped last time. Stay relaxed.

Close your eyes.
Abandon all worldly strains.
Now you see a tunnel.
Go into it.
Do stop wherever you like.
Keep moving.
Keep moving ahead.
Further.
Further and further.
Return when you don't feel like going further.
Do you see anything?'

In a barely audible and incoherent voice, Mansa said, 'I see a tall peepal tree reaching a terrace. The sun is very bright. There are three children, playing on the terrace.' Then Mansa screeched very loudly and fainted. The next moment, Shonali, Abhijit and Tushita burst into Guru Ma's room. Shonali couldn't control her sobs looking at her mother's plight. Abhijit and Tushita also fought to control their emotions.

Abhijit, in a very heavy voice asked, 'Ma, for how long will she remain tormented? Will her suffering never end? As it is, Mahashivratri is approaching, which causes her great suffering.'

Guru Ma's expression was thoughtful and mysterious. She asked, 'Does she suffer the same way every year?'

Abhijit replied peevishly, 'Yes, Ma, she suffers a migraine every year on Mahashivratri day. Could you somehow help her overcome this? We are worried for days before it comes.'

Guru Ma shut her eyes in Yog Mudra. A volunteer appeared at the door, politely indicating that they should not disturb Ma during her samadhi, and that Mansa should stay. Everyone rose to exit the room. Abhijit's gaze was fixed on Mansa, as they settled in the huge meditation quadrangle.

Mansa lay still before Ma. Even in her subconscious state, she could feel some energy and solace percolating into her from Ma's deep meditation. Soon, she had enough energy to stand on her feet and accompanied by a volunteer, she joined her family in the quadrangle. They all headed to the wooden gate and as they were crossing the gate, were handed over an appointment slip for the next past life regression session for the coming Monday afternoon. They drove back quietly without talking to each other, the silence in the car reflecting the silence in the ashram.

The excursions for the sessions was causing much physical exertion to Mansa but mentally she felt stronger to cope with the new realities haunting the canvas of her mind. She was trying to deal with new revelations and many new questions. On Monday afternoon, Mansa started for the ashram along with Tushita from her home, while Abhijit was to join them directly from office. Abhijit reached the ashram before Mansa did. Crossing the meditation hall, all three reached Guru Ma's chamber. Just like previous times, Tushita and Abhijit had to wait in the meditation hall.

Mansa prostrated before Ma and confessed, 'Ma, I feel calmer than before.'

Ma blessed her and asked her if she was ready for yet

another session. Ma assured her, 'A calm state of mind can elevate us to much higher realms in the subconscious to help us unfold the mysteries of our past.'

They both tenderly smiled at each other, as Mansa stretched down on the floor. Ma blessed her on her forehead with a feather touch and said, 'Close your eyes.

Cleanse your mind.
Clear all blocks and baggage.
Be calm.
Go back to your childhood.
Keep going back, back further back.
Try to see what causes you pain
Do you see anything?
Recall anything?

Mansa whispered, 'Yes, Ma.'

'What do you see?'

'An alley with a narrow staircase.'

'Can you climb it?'

'Yes... I am climbing with two other children.'

'Who are they?'

'My friends, Ram and Jai.'

'Who are you?'

'I am Vinya.'

Suddenly, Mansa's voice changed to that of a ten-year-old.

Guru Ma continued, 'Vinya, what are you doing?'

'I am going to play with my friends on the terrace, because we have a Mahashivratri holiday.'

'But why on the terrace and not in the compound?'

'*Ram aur Jai ko patang udana hai. Gali me subhe se Naga Sadhu Prayag mein Shivratri snan ke lie jaa rahe hai. Mujhe bhi apne friends ke saath khelna hai, mai akele thodi khelungi neeche...*' (Ram and Jai want to check on kites, plus there is a continuous stream of Naga Sadhus en route Prayag for the Mahashivratri holy bath). So, I have to be with my friends, I can't play alone in the compound.'

'What do you see now?'

'Open sky, very sunny with one or two kites.'

'What else?'

'There is a very tall peepal tree hovering over the terrace. The boys are standing under it and talking.'

'Can you hear them?'

Mansa was quiet for a while and then said, 'There are muffled voices, I can hear them say "kites" and I heard my name too.'

'What else do you see?'

'I only see the boys' backs; one is holding a roll and the other is flying a kite. Suddenly, the kite which was flying up is lost and we all scamper to the edge of the terrace to find the kite on the parapet below. There is a scuffle between the boys and they are fighting and blaming each other over the loss of the kite.'

Mansa began stuttering and then her voice faded, becoming completely inaudible. As she was lying with her eyes shut, there was a continuous stream of tears rolling down her eyes.

Guru Ma urged her, 'Mansa... Vinya, continue. You are about to cross a major threshold. Keep talking.'

Mansa continued, 'In order to calm things down, I jump

onto the parapet to pick up the kite. The parapet is weak and shaky, so I scream for help. Both the boys are busy fighting and don't pay any attention to me. Then, I look up and find a hand extended to pull me up. I hold the kite in one hand and stretch my other hand to be pulled up. I can't manage with one hand, as I may fall. I am very scared to let the kite go, but I have to.' Mansa started wailing like a ten-year-old child. 'I have to let go off the kite and clutch the hand very tightly. I am even more frightened, as I can hear the boys fighting. My grip is loosening and the noise they are making is increasing and suddenly the hand holding me drops me...'

'My forehead hits something sharp on the ground... blood, blood everywhere. I am writhing in unbearable, agonizing pain and no one comes to help me. I keep lying in a pool of blood. I've fallen in a desolate back alley. Terrified, both the boys have left me to die.'

Mansa was sobbing uncontrollably, her voice choking every now and then, as if reliving the pain of the past and then, mercifully, fainted. A very worried Abhijit entered with Tushita. They both uttered a quick pranam to Ma and looked helplessly at Mansa.

Ma blessed them and informed them, 'Mansa might take longer to gain consciousness, as today she was able to break the barrier to travel to the past and unravel the cause of her migraine in this life. Her untimely accidental death in her past life was excruciatingly painful and slow. She carries these memories in this life too and they surface every year at the same time to haunt her.'

Abhijit was finding it hard to come to terms with this

sort of reality. For him everything was here and now. Who has seen the future and who can ever know the past? But he could not easily dismiss what Guru Ma had just said either and a cold chill hit his spine.

Unlike the previous times, they were not asked to leave Ma's chamber. Guru Ma wanted to ensure that after her trauma, Mansa was fine. Quite a while later, Mansa started showing some signs of regaining consciousness. Abhijit noticed that her milky pink complexion had turned pale and dull. All her exuberance and energy had completely evaporated. Her psychic trips to invisible lands of the past life seemed to have turned her lifeless. As Mansa sat up, Guru Ma asked her how she felt.

Mansa experienced a deep tranquillity, which she had never felt before. She smiled faintly at everyone and said that she felt better. As they both prostrated before Guru Ma for her blessings, something most unanticipated happened. Guru Ma looked at them both, first at Mansa and then at Abhijit. And then very gently, she warned them that they needed to exercise extra caution in their lives and prophesized, 'Mansa is destined to face the fate of an unnatural death at the hands of the same person in this life too. The one who pushed her and the other one who tried saving her have already entered her life.'

Mansa's smile suddenly disappeared and her mind travelled to Rajan. The anguish he had caused her by dropping her so casually from his life had caused her to die a million deaths. The mental hurt inflicted by Rajan had temporarily receded behind the pain of the fall from the terrace and her consequent bleeding to death. It resurfaced with a bang.

The only two men she could think of in her present life

were Rajan and Abhijit. She thought how lucky she would be to die at the hands of either, as they were the only men she had been close to in this life and whom she had been most intimate with. Abhijit, who loved her more than anything else, and Rajan, the love of her life, who she had loved more than anything else.

At last she managed to say, 'I want to talk to Ma alone for a minute, if you two don't mind.'

Tushita and Abhijit left the chamber and Mansa said to Ma, 'I have a confession to make. I've been married for over twenty years. I can say in all truth and honesty that I have been truly in love with my husband as the one and only person in my life, but suddenly last year, something happened that was beyond my control and unintentionally I got drawn to a person whom I have never met. I have been let down and feel deeply hurt and betrayed by that man. I am failing to get over it as there was something in that relationship which was beyond my normal comprehension. I have no reason and logic that can explain why—with a husband like Abhijit by my side—I would get attracted to another man and that too, after so many years of a normal married life. I am not able to move on. And now you say that I will die the same way again.'

Ma did not react and Mansa realized that she was already in samadhi. As she had moved a few steps towards the exit door, Ma gently called her, 'Come here. I want to say one last thing.'

Mansa stopped and turned to face Guru Ma.

Ma said, 'There is a connection. Past life connection, a karmic connection,' and she was back into samadhi.

Mansa asked, 'How can I break this karmic cycle?'

There was no answer.

15

The Gullies of Childhood

'Nobody deserves your tears, but whoever deserves them will not make you cry.'

—Gabriel García Márquez

AS THEY RODE home, Mansa felt more vulnerable and nostalgic. She was missing her grandmother, her parents and her sisters too. She remembered how she had been pampered as a child by everyone.

Her eldest sister, Mala, had always looked after her like a second mother. Her grandmother and other sister, Meera, had also been like mothers to her. In all, she had had four mothers. So there had been no opportunity to experience, learn or experiment with life first-hand. She had been destined to a life where there was no self-learning from trial and error; rather, she was given a tailor-made, cocooned life, altered to perfection based on the experiences of the others, so that she did not have to go through any bad experiences herself. Almost every person in her life in the past and the present had organized her life, until it got physically more and more comfortable. She was treated as though she was the most precious crystal, incapable of bearing even the slightest stress. She had always cherished this, until she had entered the fourth decade of her life.

She had always been kept like a prized possession by her grandmother, in a family in which very few children had survived. She had never been allowed outside the home by herself, and had been closely guarded, as though the outside world had only one agenda on mind—to harm her. This overzealousness from her family had resulted in Mansa being naive, impractical and inexperienced on many counts. She had missed out on fumbling and falling and even discovering the simple truths of life related to her own sexuality. She had never experienced the usual pleasures of other growing adolescents.

Retrospectively, it still hurt to reminisce how in school as well as in college, she had always been ridiculed and side-lined by her classmates, who gossiped about her as someone who didn't understand anything. She still blushed and trembled when she remembered a boy from a senior class in school, had mustered the courage to give her a love note. Instead of feeling special, she had felt morally indignant and had given it to her mother, who was a teacher in her school, without understanding or considering his feelings. From that day on, she always found herself friendless and lonely in school, as she was labelled as a girl who couldn't be trusted and was a teacher's mole.

When any boy showed an interest in her, her headstrong

sisters dealt with them very severely. Mala had been one of the most popular, charismatic and iconic girls in school and the neighbourhood. She was not only confident and smart, but even enjoyed their parents' confidence, unlike Mansa. Not only this, her eldest sister had managed to have a boyfriend right under their mother's nose in school. She was a young rebel, who believed in challenging everything and doing things her way. At a rather early age, she had settled into early matrimony with her third boyfriend, leaving Mansa's care in Meera's hands.

Meera, though much less dominating than Mala, took charge of her younger sister rather zealously. But, the most beautiful memories Mansa possessed were those of her grandmother, her Dadi. She had been a major influence her childhood. If she had to describe her childhood in one word, it would be 'Dadi'. She still had a vivid picture of her grandmother in her mind, as the head of their clan. She would always be perched in a dignified manner on a bare wooden divan on the veranda, with a hookah in her hand. She was looked up to as a leader by the displaced Punjabis of western Punjab, which is now Pakistan. She had once owned vast stretches of land, all lost in the 1947 partition of India. Despite this, she had coped pretty well with life, without complaining. When her family took shelter in a refugee colony, she had become a mentor, counsellor, legal advisor and religious head to all the refugees living nearby. Many people of the community continuously thronged to their house to consult her on a diverse range of issues and hers was accepted as the last word in her community.

Mansa's mind wandered to that dreadful day, which she had tried to shut out from her mind. Till now a frozen memory in the cold storage of her mind, it was waiting to be thawed.

The second Indo-Pak war had just ended. Lieutenant-General A.A.K. Niazi, supreme commander of the Pakistani army in East Pakistan, had surrendered to General Jagjit Singh Arora of the Indian Allied Forces. It was still the talk of the town even though it had occurred almost two months ago. Mansa, at barely five or six, Meera, a little over eight, and a ten-year-old Mala were quite a handful. It was early morning. Most of the household, especially the children, were all fast asleep. There was a lot of buzz and activity at home as it was a very special day. Her Dadi was in complete control of the house, her strong, strident voice commanding the women to go through a basic checklist of dos and don'ts. Mansa's three buas, along with their friends, were home. Mansa, with half-shut eyes, tossed and turned in bed, as the cacophony of women was getting unbearable. She was also keenly aware of the aroma of laddus, matthis, and many other snacks that Ramesh, their cook, was busy preparing under Dadi's tight vigil. It was no small event. The ladies were all preparing to leave for their annual ritual bath, the Maha Snan Kumbh for two days, beginning from Mahashivratri.

Every year, for generations, all the senior women of the family had followed this tradition of sacred snan on Mahashivratri. It was not only a ritualistic bath, but also a celebratory picnic and shopping spree. To the women, it was the most exciting time of the year. First, they all gathered at Allahabad Prayag for the religious dip and from there they moved to Vishwanath Baba in Kashi. Besides kirtan, there was also dancing and merrymaking on the way. Eating, shopping, gossiping, chatting and dancing were all intrinsic to the spirit of Kumbh and the religious fervour.

Mansa had suddenly felt a choking sensation, not caused by the aromas or noise, but by intense pain, which had started emanating from her temples and spread to one side of her skull. The pain kept increasing. Then, she saw a dark narrow staircase, heard incoherent voices. She saw an alley and an old peepal tree and she screamed. The pain rose and rose, till she could take it no more and passed out, only to be woken later with various medications.

She had regained consciousness after almost five hours. As her eyes fluttered open, she saw Dadi's pale, worried face leaning over her and caressing her forehead lovingly. Despite all the fuss and preparation, it had been impossible for Dadi to leave her in that state. Mansa's eyeballs scanned the room to find only her Dadi and parents around. The other pilgrims had left in the mini bus hired for the occasion. As long ago as she could recall, it was the first time that she had seen her Dadi miss the yearly ritual of Kumbh snan on Mahashivratri. Notwithstanding all her dharma, karma and punya, penance, the three sisters were her Dadi's centre of the universe.

From that year on, every Mahashivratri morning, Mansa encountered the same pain, which she dreaded in the days before the sacred occasion. Although a very holy day of the Hindu calendar, it was a day of endless misery for her. No matter how much treatment her father tried—allopathy, homeopathy, Ayurveda, Unani, naturopathy, acupressure, holistic healing— nothing worked out for his ladli, as he fondly called Mansa.

Years passed, with no escape from the migraine that

recurred relentlessly at the same time. A doctor suggested that matrimony might cure Mansa. So her marriage to Abhijit was fixed by traditional matchmakers in their closely knit endogamous community. But the migraine attacks only got worse after her marriage.

Once married, the centuries-old tradition of her family sprouted in her heart too. Year after year, her yearning for a dip on Mahahivratri day was getting stronger and stronger. During her migraines, she was now being cared for and pampered by her own husband, just like her Dadi had always done. She had noticed Abhijit's eyes filled with tears many times when she whimpered in pain.

Abhijit's world was made of tangible logic and reasoning. She had expressed her desire to Abhijit to be taken to the Mahashivratri Kumbh, but he would have none of it. To even consider taking her anywhere in her terrible state and that too for a snan instead of taking her to a doctor, he would have to throw his education in a bin first, he would say. To him it was illogical and irrational. He always maintained that God lives in our hearts and kindness is the true religion.

But that year was different. She pleaded, 'Promise me that you will take me for the Mahashivratri Kumbh snan this year. It's on 12 February this year. Let's go please.'

Keeping her health in mind, Abhijit was not able to say no this time and promised her a ritual bath. Mansa breathed a deep sigh of relief just as the car came to a halt in their building's parking space.

16

Prophecy of the Past: The Chakra Continues

'I come out alone on my way to my tryst. But who is this that follows me in the silent dark? I move aside to avoid his presence but I escape him not.'

—Gurudeb Rabindranath Tagore

ABHIJIT BROUGHT BACK home a visibly more shaken Mansa, who was much more adamant on a Kumbh *snan* on Mahashivratri than ever before. He was sure that she would not listen to any of his logic and he would have to yield to her demand.

They were well into February by now. Mala and Meera, who had come to see her from the US when they heard of her illness, made her feel much better. All three of them had a happy reunion and laughed and wept one at the same time over their departed parents and childhood memories. They had left for the US just a few days back and devoid of their laughter, the house seemed very empty again.

Shivratri was just a fortnight away. Abhijit made bookings for the snan and their stay. Mansa seemed to be getting better in spirit and strength. Abhijit's constant care and his efforts to take her to the Kumbh made her deeply content. The night before they were to leave for Allahabad she felt very blissful. For almost a month now, she had been insisting on sleeping between Shonali and Abhijit. When her sisters were around, she had done the same, sleeping between them to draw comfort from their presence.

The hurtful pangs in her heart, caused by the loss of Rajan, were no better, but somehow her life was slowly drifting ahead towards normality. She was again thinking a lot about her Dadi. She felt that a dip in the holy water of Prayag would certainly help cure her hurt and battered soul.

In her sleep, she was again tormented by a deluge of emotions. She saw the same dream she had seen in London, when Rajan had blocked her—she saw a ceaseless ocean, without beginning or end. She was terrified, feeling that she was drowning. She wanted to hold on to something or someone, but there was nothing. She found herself alone. Nervously, she looked around for someone to extend a helping hand. She expectantly and longingly looked at Rajan, but he turned away. Further anguished and terrified, she looked at Abhijit, but he did not pay heed to her cry for help.

She woke up screaming and perspiring, waking up Abhijit and Shonali too. Mansa could not sleep after that.

Early next morning, she gave Shonali a tight hug and left for the airport with Abhijit to catch their flight to Allahabad. They reached Prayag, early in the morning, on the day of the Kumbh. Abhijit wanted to do his best for her. He had hired a wooden boat and they were rowed by the boatman to the confluence of the Ganga, Yamuna and the mythical Saraswati rivers.

The bright sun overhead, despite the canopy on the boat, made the pain of her migraine sharper, causing Mansa to feel dizzier. As Mansa had strongly refused a motorboat in favour of the centuries-old traditional way of going for a dip in a wooden boat, Abhijit had little choice but to comply. It took them over an hour of rowing to reach the confluence. Despite her pain, Mansa appeared brighter and radiated a happiness, which Abhijit had not seen in ages. He extended his hand to help her stand in the boat.

Mansa wanted Abhijit to go into the water first. Finally, holding on to the boatman with one hand and gripping Abhijit tightly with the other, she alighted from the boat. Abhijit then held both her hands, and chanting shlokas and mantras, they took several dips together.

Mansa appeared exhausted after the dips. Holding her firmly and looking skywards, Abhijit said, 'Oh God, let Mansa be my wife for all my lives.'

Mansa looked at him in disbelief. A man who could never even bring himself to say 'I love you' had said it all today. Guilt again enveloped her.

Mansa felt scared and nervous, as she secretly wanted to send prayers for prosperity and happiness for Rajan, as she still thought of him as her true love, even though his brusque behaviour had devastated her. Whatever had been his intent or feelings, the fact of the matter was that she had loved him most intensely.

She could see the same love in Abhijit's eyes for her. Suddenly, she felt giddy and her grip on Abhijit's hand loosened. The boat by now had drifted a little further away. Holding her tight, Abhijit tried wading towards the boat with her. The level of the water started rising too. As he reached the boat, the boatman tried to balance and straighten the boat. Abhijit had no choice, but to climb in first, so he could help Mansa climb into the boat. Firmly holding her hand, he hoisted himself into the boat. Suddenly, there was a jostle and thud from a nearby boat, shaking their boat violently. Abhijit's grip over Mansa's hand loosened.

With an ear-splitting splash, Mansa fell into the water without much struggle. As she fell, Guru Ma's words echoed in her ears—the person who was responsible for her unnatural death in her previous life would be responsible for her unnatural death in this life too. And the Kaal Chakra would continue. For the Kaal Chakra to be broken, she would have to be saved by the other man and would have to die a natural death.

Mansa was suddenly engulfed by darkness. Abhijit and the boatman jumped in after her, but it was too late. The mighty surge of water had pulled Mansa into its depths, in a final fatal embrace.

The beginning and the end are two sides of the same coin.
In a circle, there is no beginning and no end.

Look out for Mansa's trials and tribulations in her next life in the sequel.

Acknowledgements

31 *Miles* is dedicated to you. It is your story and mine. *31 Miles* is dedicated to the unsung and uncelebrated common hero that lives in each one of us. Life becomes more beautiful and meaningful when we are able to rise above our personal desires to reach out to the ones who need us within or outside of our families. It celebrates the spirit of family and friends that look after the needs of special children and terminally ill. Unknowingly their lives undergo change and become stories of heroic patience. God may give us all strength to become more humane.

Mummy, Papa, many thanks to you. I would not be holding this pen if it were not for your love and blessings. My brothers,Deepak and Priyankar you always add to my strength. My support system: my husband Vijay, son Parantap, daughter Jugnu and last but not the least my mother-in-law.

This book would not have been what it is without the repeated readings and creative criticism from my daughter Jugnu.

A book is a long journey. You need people to guide you through. It's one thing to write a book and another to make it reach your table. I was lucky to find support of many friends who supported me through this journey. Thanks, Bhaskar Bhatt, Rahul Saini, Somak Ghosal, Dr Geeta Chaudhary, Vanita Yadav, Rashmi Singh Anshu Prakash, Madhup Mohta, Prof. Suman Sharma, Kamayni, Deeksha, Jai, Urvashi, Vimla Mehra and Farhat Shehzad. There definitely are many others who have stood by me and believed in me— Thank you friends.

I must make a special mention of the media personality and real life hero, Rajiv Makhni. Even when preoccupied, he takes out time to support for our issue based programs. I am honored by his rendition of this book's foreword. Thank you, Rajiv.

Last but not the least, I would like to convey my gratitude to the famous film director and writer, Imitiaz Ali. Imtiaz's cinema has been a true favourite of mine—always creative and soul stirring. I'm grateful for his valuable time to review *31 Miles*, and make my debut novel extra special. Thank you, Imtiaz.